the
TRAPDOOR
mysteries

THIEF IN THE NIGHT

THE TRAPDOOR MYSTERY SERIES

the
TRAPDOOR
mysteries

THIEF IN THE NIGHT

ABIE LONGSTAFF
Illustrations by James Brown

Orion
Children's Books

ORION CHILDREN'S BOOKS

First published in Great Britain in 2019 by Hodder and Stoughton

1 3 5 7 9 10 8 6 4 2

A CIP catalogue record for this book
is available from the British Library.

ISBN 978-1-5101-042-42

Printed and bound by
CPI Group (UK) Ltd, Croydon, CR0 4YY

The paper and board used in this book are
made from wood from responsible sources.

Orion Children's Books
An imprint of
Hachette Children's Group
Part of Hodder and Stoughton
Carmelite House
50 Victoria Embankment
London EC4Y 0DZ

An Hachette UK Company
www.hachette.co.uk
www.hachettechildrens.co.uk

The Secret Library's Rules:

There will be only one Secret Keeper
in each generation.

The Secret Keeper must be
under the age of thirteen.

The Keeper must guard the secret of
the library and the information within.

Talking is permitted.

CHAPTER ONE

Tally the servant girl shivered and wrapped her raggedy cardigan more tightly around her body. It was early morning and she was out in the snowy grounds of Mollett Manor, looking for firewood. She lifted her lamp higher and scanned the forest floor.

She nudged her pinafore pocket. 'Hello? Aren't you going to help me?'

Squill, her squirrel friend, popped his head out, gave one sniff of the cold air and dived back down again.

'Come on!' Tally insisted. 'You're the one with the super-thick winter coat.' She reached her fingers in and poked his soft fur. He squeaked and shot out of her pocket, somersaulting in the air and landing on a low branch.

'Show off!' said Tally, laughing as she added a twig to her basket.

There was a rustle in the bushes, then a loud **squawk!** Tally jumped. *What was that?*

Squill hopped down from his branch and darted ahead into the dark trees to investigate, his body curving on the snow like a red wave.

'Wait for me!' cried Tally. She pushed the branches aside, yelping as snow tumbled off and ran down the back of her neck. In front of her, Squill stopped short and took a wary step backward. There in the low brambles was a huge owl. He was white with brown speckles and his wide eyes stared at Tally in fright.

'There, there,' said Tally softly. The owl was caught. It looked like he had fallen from the tree above, and his wing was trapped in the thorny branches.

'Stay back, Squill,' she told the squirrel.
Squirrels were a very tasty snack for tawny owls
like this one. Squill snorted as if to say, *Duh!
What do you think I'm doing?* and dashed up on
to a nearby tree to watch.

Slowly Tally inched forward, closer and closer
to the owl. She crouched down on her knees in
the snowy ground, her lamp by her side.

'I'm going to free you,' she said in a low voice.
In the soft lamplight her fingers gently pulled
at the tangled brambles, untwisting them from
the owl's feathers. 'Sorry!' she said as a thorn
got caught and the owl jerked back in fright.
Tally continued to murmur kindly to him and
gradually he calmed down.

'Nearly done …' Tally pulled aside the final
bramble. '… There! You're free!'

The owl hopped out of the branches. His left
wing was ragged, the feathers ripped apart by
thorns. The owl tried to fly but could only flutter
up to a low branch. From there he climbed along
using his claws to grip.

'We need to keep an eye on that wing,' Tally told him. 'Rest for now and I'll be back to check on you later today.'

The owl closed his eyes and tucked his head under his good wing.

Squill dived down from the tree and landed on Tally's shoulder.

'Now,' said Tally. 'I've lit the fires, polished the hall, swept the cloister and made a whole pile of cherry biscuits.' She counted her completed chores off on her fingers. 'And the sun's not even up! We should be able to sneak to the Secret Library before anyone else is awake.'

But just as she turned to go, there was a shriek from an upstairs window. It was Lady Beatrice.

'Tally!' she screamed. 'Help!'

'I saw it again!' Lady Beatrice sobbed into a handkerchief.

Tally rushed around Lady Beatrice's bedroom, lighting the lamps. She picked up Lady Beatrice's pillows and tucked them behind her mistress.

'There you go,' she said, in a soft voice, pulling the covers over Lady Beatrice's shivering shoulders.

'It was just like before. A tiny ghost, all grey. And it was right there!' Lady Beatrice pointed to her window sill.

For the last week, Lady Beatrice had barely slept. She was certain the manor house was haunted, and she'd woken Tally up nearly every night, convinced she had seen a ghost. Tally didn't believe in ghosts. Not even the Secret Library, with all its books on the mysteries of the world, had any information on them – Tally knew because she'd tried to research them.

'Ghosts aren't real, Lady Beatrice,' Tally said gently.

'Oh, but I heard it! In the middle of the night something tapped at my bathroom window. I ran to see but by the time I got there, it had gone.' Lady Beatrice's eyes were wide and her cheeks were pale. 'And then this morning I saw … I saw … the ghost!' She burst into tears.

Tally patted her shoulder. Poor Lady Beatrice. Until last week, she'd been happy for the first time in ages. She adored her puppy, Lord William (nicknamed Widdles by Tally, due to his many unfortunate 'accidents'), and she had even taken up photography in order to record his cuteness on film. Mollett Manor was slowly filling with Lady Beatrice's black and white images of Widdles chewing sticks, rolling in the mud and chasing his tail. To everyone's surprise, Lady Beatrice was a fine photographer. She seemed to have an instinct for capturing interesting angles and shards of light.

But lately, with so many night-time scares and such little sleep, Lady Beatrice hadn't taken a single photo. She carried her camera everywhere with her, like a child with a teddy bear, but she had stopped using it. Now, sitting in bed with her covers up to her chin, she seemed so fragile, like a china doll. She poked a limp hand out of the blankets to stroke the camera. It was her pride and joy, a dark mahogany camera with a shiny brass fitting on the top for viewing the shot. It was the latest thing and came all the way from Denmark.[1]

Lady Beatrice yawned.

'I'm so sleepy,' she said, pulling the camera to her chest. 'I think I'm just going to stay in bed today.'

'But it's going to be a lovely day,' said Tally, 'and you promised the publisher you'd take photos of William, remember?'

Lady Beatrice had agreed to photograph Widdles for Lord Mollett's book. He'd started writing it last summer, when Widdles had arrived at the manor house. It was called **ETIQUETTE IN CANINES: Bone or Bone China?**

The publisher, Messrs Tweet, Lotts & Hope wanted lots of photos of dogs in various poses,

---

[1] Lady Beatrice owned one of the world's first 35mm film cameras. Many people at the time still used plate cameras, which were heavy and cumbersome, or box Brownie cameras, which were a simple design made of leather-covered card.

to illustrate the pages. They had greatly admired Lady Beatrice's photographs of Widdles and had specially asked her to take the pictures for the book. It would be Lady Beatrice's first paid job as a photographer; in fact, it would be her first paid job ever.

'Oh, Tally. I don't think I can today. I'm so tired.'

'Just have a little nap. Then when you feel ready I'll help you.'

'I don't know,' said Lady Beatrice. 'I still feel all shaken up. I'd give anything to get rid of that ghost at my window,' she sighed. 'Anything!'

Tally frowned. This 'ghost' was becoming a real problem. She opened the window and leaned out to investigate. On the outside sill were little prints in the snow. Lady Beatrice was right – something had been there! What could it have been? The prints weren't like a bird's – Tally pictured bird

16

footprints, all spindly like trees.

They weren't like a squirrel's
either – Squill had paws. He
held them up for Tally to
see their base. They were
kind of oval, with pads.
He had four fingers on his
front paws, and five toes on
his back paws.

Tally looked at the prints on the sill
again. They were longer and thinner than
Squill's, with four fingers and a thumb. They
looked like … Tally frowned … tiny hands!

She stood back. It couldn't really be a ghost,
could it?

'Look, Tally. I'm trembling all over!' said Lady Beatrice, pointing at her goose pimples. 'You see! It must be a ghost. They do say phantoms bring the shivers.'

'Lady Beatrice, you are shivering because it's winter, not because of a ghost,' Tally explained as she shut the window.

'Oh yes,' said Lady Beatrice. 'I remember now. Lucky we can all stay tucked up inside in the warmth.' She snuggled deeper down into bed, her camera beside her.

Tally smiled and left her to sleep. Maybe now she could make a visit to the Secret Library … if she could get past Mrs Sneed the housekeeper and Mr Bood the butler.

'There you are!' snapped Mrs Sneed from her armchair by the stove in the kitchen, where she was snaffling her way through the cherry biscuits Tally had made early that morning.

'Huh. About time, Twooly,' grumbled Mr Bood (he could never remember her name).

'We've even had to make our own tea.' He lifted a cup and slurped it noisily.

Tally groaned silently. *Here we go again*, she said inside her head. More chores.

'You need to clear snow from the top of the trees, Tally.'

'Blow on the rose petals to warm the flowers, Toolley!'

'Wipe the windows every two minutes so they don't steam up, Tally!'

'Hunt harder for strawberries, Twilly. They must be growing somewhere!'

'Mr Bood,' Tally said, trying not to sigh out loud, 'there aren't any strawberries in the winter. Remember? It's too cold for them to grow.'

'It's lovely and warm,' Mr Bood insisted, stretching his toes towards the fire.

'Yes,' Tally answered him patiently. 'That's because you are sitting inside by the fire with a cup of tea. Outside, it is cold.'

'Stop being lazy, Tally,' added Mrs Sneed, through a mouthful of cake. 'Those windows won't wipe themselves, you know.'

'Looks like we won't be able to go to the library quite yet, Squill,' said Tally as she carried a bucket down the hallway. She climbed the stairs to the blue drawing room and lifted her cloth to wipe the first window.

All through her chores, Tally thought about the ghost. It wasn't real. It couldn't be. But what could have climbed so high in the dark just to sit on the window sill? As she made her way along the corridor from the west wing to the east, wiping every window, Tally discovered something else. There were no footprints on any of the other window sills. The ghost – or whatever it was – seemed to have only visited Lady Beatrice's room.

Tally dusted along the top of the new row of doggy portraits. Here was Widdles with his head to one side, almost grinning at the camera. There he was with his head stuck in the gate, and yes – here was Tally's favourite photo. She called it *Widdles Confused by Snow*. It was a black and white shot[2] of the puppy sunk up to his chest. He was licking the snow surrounding him, and his eyes looked up at the camera as if to say, *Huh? What is this weird cold stuff?*

Lady Beatrice had taken it last month. She'd been so full of excitement then, dancing around the house happily with her new hobby. But now, now she was in bed, worried and upset, not taking any photos at all.

[2] The first colour photograph was taken in 1861, using red, green and blue filters.

Squill poked Tally's leg with a paw. He'd swept the dust into a neat pile ready for her to gather up.

'Oh sorry, Squill! I was lost in thought.' She held out the dustpan and Squill swept the dust in with his red tail. 'Thanks.'

At the end of the corridor were Lord and Lady Beatrice's bedrooms. Lord Mollett's was to the north, overlooking the grand drive, and Lady Beatrice's was to the south with a view of the gardens. They were the same rooms they'd had growing up as brother and sister. Lord Mollett's door was ajar and Tally could see him sitting on the chaise longue. Her heart skipped a beat.

She'd recently discovered something. Something about her past. There was a chance, a possibility that Lord Mollett could be her father. Tally felt a thrill run through her every time she thought about it. She'd never known who her father was. Her mother, Martha, had brought Tally to Mollett Manor nine years ago, when Tally was only two years old. But Ma had fallen at the cliff edge, fallen down the crumbly rocks to the sea below, and Tally hadn't seen her since. Maybe she was gone for ever. But if – if – Lord Mollett really was her father, he could help Tally find out for sure. Together, maybe, they could even find Ma! Maybe …

Tally shook her head. She had to stop herself from having yet another daydream where Lord Mollett welcomed her as his daughter. 'My little girl!' he'd cry (in her imagination) and he'd open his arms wide.

She backed away from the door as quickly as she could and scurried back down the corridor. She didn't breathe again until she reached the west wing. Opening the door of the blue drawing room, she slipped in and Squill jumped up on to her shoulder.

'I'm not certain he's my father,' she said. 'I can't prove it … yet.'

Squill put his little paws around her neck to hug her tight.

'Thanks, Squill.' Tally stroked him, burying her fingers into his warm red fur.

'We have to find out if it's really true,' said Tally. 'We have to find proof. Then … and only then … I'll talk to Lord Mollett. And I know where to start searching.'

Squill jumped up excitedly.

'That's right, Squill. The Secret Library. Come on.'

'Tally!' Mrs Sneed's voice bellowed from the kitchen. 'We need some more of those cherry biscuits. Right now!'

CHAPTER TWO

Tally kneaded biscuit dough on the marble
kitchen counter, her fingers squishing into the
gooey mixture. She loved making these cherry
biscuits. There was something about feeling the
dough, pressing it and shaping it in her hands,
that helped her think. The recipe was an old
one – it had been stuck on the kitchen wall for as
long as Tally had been living at the manor. But
Tally didn't even need to look at the instructions
any more. She knew the recipe off by heart – the
biscuits were Lord Mollett's favourite snack. *My*

father's biscuits, thought Tally, followed by *Stop that! Don't think about it!* Squill sneakily pinched a bit of dough to nibble. He loved Tally's biscuits. Especially the cherries – they were the best bit.

There was a snuffle from the top of Tally's feet. It was Widdles. He had taken to lying right on Tally's feet for warmth. He stayed there, balanced on her shoes, even when Tally shuffled across the kitchen to fetch a baking tray.

'Ruff,' said Widdles, and Squill tossed him down a bit of dough. The puppy stared at it on the floor.

'You're supposed to eat it,' Tally explained, but Widdles just sniffed at it suspiciously. Then he put his nose right on to it, squishing it flat. When he lifted his face, the bit of dough was stuck to the end of his nose. His big brown eyes focused in, going cross-eyed as he tried to look at it.

'You'll have to rescue him, Squill,' said Tally. 'I don't have a free hand.'

Squill did not look happy about that plan. Luckily Brie, Tally's rat friend, appeared, scurrying across the floor on her teeny rat paws. She spied the squashed dough on Widdles's nose, picked it off and ate it up in one gulp.

'Thanks, Brie!' Tally said. She smiled at the rat. Last summer, Tally had rescued Brie from nasty Colin – the animal kidnapper – as well as a budgie, a gecko, three hamsters, four rabbits, one hundred ants and the Mollett Manor bees.

All the animals lived at the manor, some in secret corners, some in the stables. Tally lifted her eyes to see the crested gecko darting across the kitchen wall towards the oven for warmth. She wiggled her dough-covered fingers in a wave.

Widdles licked the remaining crumbs off his

nose and, for the first time, tasted the delicious cherry biscuits of Mollett Manor. His eyes sparkled and at that moment, a bright ray of sunshine shot in through the kitchen window, lighting up his face. Tally laughed as she slid the biscuits into the oven and closed the door. 'Lady Beatrice should be here, taking photos of you,' she said to the puppy. 'Let's see if we can persuade her to get up.'

'Wuff!' he said happily, and he trotted off down the hall, only falling over his ears twice. *Well, at least, he's making progress*, thought Tally. *That's better than me.* She hadn't found any more clues to the 'ghost', and she hadn't even found time to go to the Secret Library. Inside the library was Martha's diary, and in the diary there could be answers – answers to confirm all her hunches about her father. Tally shook her head and cleared her mind. *Stop that!* For now, her priority had to be Lady Beatrice.

'No! Stay still! Lord William! Stay still!' cried Lady Beatrice.

Tally had finally persuaded her out of bed
and all the way to the fountain in the courtyard,
where she was now desperately trying to keep
Widdles in one place.

'Lord William Horatio Mollett! Stop moving!'
Lady Beatrice slumped in despair. 'It's not
working! All I want is for William to look regal
and elegant, imposing yet kindly. I can't even
manage that.'

Tally frowned as Widdles
rolled in the snow, barking at
a leaf. Regal wasn't exactly
the right word for him.

There came a cough from over
by the fountain. It was Mr Bood. He was leaning
casually against the statue, with an unnatural
grin set on his face.

'I am available for photographs,' he announced.
Then he posed with his nose in the air.

'Oh I do need you, Mr Bood!' said Lady
Beatrice. The butler's face lit up, and he sucked
in his tummy, ready for a starring role. 'Yes,'
continued Lady Beatrice, 'I need you to help

with Lord William. I can't get him to sit on the stool and hold this fork. Could you …?' She handed Mr Bood the cutlery and his face fell. He lifted Widdles on to his stool and, crouching down behind it, tried to fit the fork into Widdles's slobbery mouth.

Lady Beatrice made a makeshift square shape out of the index fingers and thumbs of both hands and squinted through it. 'Lower … lower, Mr Bood. Yes, that's good. I can't see you at all now.'

Tally heard a muttering from behind the stool. Then a flump! as Mr Bood lost his balance and fell over into the snow.

'Wuff!' said Widdles. He jumped off to join in the new game of 'fall in the snow' before Lady Beatrice could take the photograph.

'Oh no! I have to get the picture before the postman comes to collect the film. And my hands are still shaking from seeing that ghost.' Lady Beatrice's voice caught. 'I shouldn't have taken this job! I don't think I'll ever be a proper photographer.' Tally could sense she was going to break down in tears any moment. She took the golden fork from Mr Bood. It glinted and glistened in the sunshine.

'Ruff!' Widdles shook his head vigorously. Mud flew off on to the snow and Lady Beatrice jumped back.

There was a deep laugh from behind her and Tally's heart leaped. There in the doorway was Lord Mollett. He grinned at her kindly. Her tummy dropped. *Does he know? Does he recognise me*? She shook her head to clear the thoughts. *Stop it!*

'I'll help too,' he told his sister.

'Oh, thank you!' said Lady Beatrice, as Lord Mollett lifted the puppy in his arms and put him back on the stool by the fountain. Widdles barked and wriggled, spraying muddy snow everywhere. Tally wiped his fur with her pinafore.

'Stay there,' she whispered. 'If you just keep still for one minute you can have a cherry biscuit.'

Widdles pricked up his ears at the words, and his eyes sparkled.

'He looks wonderful!' cried Lady Beatrice. For a moment she sounded like herself again.

Tally stood back and smiled. Widdles did look very cute. Yes, he still had bits of stick in the corners of his mouth and mud on his whiskers, but his eyes were bright and happy, and the golden fork shone in his mouth.

Lady Beatrice looked through her polished brass view finder, held her breath and pressed the shutter release.

'There,' she said, leaning against her brother in exhaustion. 'I hope that's good enough,' she said. 'I'm not at my best, I'm afraid.'

'You're doing splendidly,' he said, kindly.

Lady Beatrice removed the film from the

camera and put it in a special canister. 'I think I'll go and lie down now,' she said.

There was a whistle from the gate and the postman waved from behind the bars.

'Just in time,' said Tally, waving at the postman to wait a moment. She took the canister from Lady Beatrice to the scullery and put it in a parcel, then ran across the lawn to the heavy gate.

'Morning, miss!' said the postman. 'Here's something for her ladyship.' He took the parcel and handed Tally a card addressed directly to Lady Beatrice.

'You read it, Tally,' said Lady Beatrice, when Tally brought it back to her. 'I've no idea where my glasses have gone.'

'They're on your head, your ladyship,' said Tally.

'Oh, I can't be bothered to fetch them from all the way up there!' exclaimed Lady Beatrice. 'Just read it to me.'

Tally read:

If there's something strange
in your manor house,
If there's something weird,
and it's not a mouse,
Whom is one going to call?

Madame Sage, the Medium.

Company motto: Don't spook
till you're spooken to!

'Ohhh!' cried Lady Beatrice, in relief. 'That's just what I need! I'm going to telephone her right away.' She rushed off inside. Tally frowned, lost in thought.

'What is it, Tally?' Lord Mollett asked her.

'I don't know,' she answered. 'Something doesn't feel right. That card arriving was such a coincidence. And why was it addressed to Lady Beatrice specifically?'

Lord Mollett smiled at her. 'Well if anyone can figure out what's going on, it's you,' he said.

His voice grew soft. 'You know, Tally, you remind me so much of someone I used to know.'

Tally stilled. *Was it Ma? Was that who he was talking about?* She bit her lip. It was so hard being around Lord Mollett these days! She just wanted to blurt out the words *I think you're my father*. But she couldn't. Not yet.

'We really need your help, Tally,' he continued. 'My poor sister has been having a rough time of things recently. And, when she's upset, I'm upset too.' He shook his head. 'Family, eh? Lucky I never had children myself. I'd worry all the time!'

Tally's blood ran cold.

'Yes, yes, it's for the best,' said Lord Mollett. 'Anyway …' He made his voice gruff, as if to chase unhappy thoughts away. 'I have to add a bit more to my chapter on sleeping habits,' he said. 'Any chance you could help me put in some facts?'

Tally nodded. She could barely lift her head.

'Thank you. I've no idea where you get all your information from, but it's very useful.'

For a moment Tally felt a glow – he thought she was useful! But then she was cold all over again.

It's for the best echoed in her mind.

'Hmm?' Lord Mollett was waiting for her to answer.

Tally wasn't allowed to tell anyone about the Secret Library. 'Oh, just books,' she answered quickly.

'Are you all right, Tally?'

'Yes. Yes.' She was desperate to get away. 'I'll come and find you with some information this afternoon.'

'Biscuits too?' added Lord Mollett hopefully. And, for a moment, his eyes looked just like Widdles's.

CHAPTER THREE

It's for the best.

It's for the best.

Tally was so upset. All she could think about was getting to the Secret Library, where she could hide away. Squill nuzzled into her neck as she slipped into the woods.

There was a hoot from a branch above her head.

'Oh, Mr Owl!' Tally had forgotten about him! She shook her own worries from her mind and moved closer to look at his wing. He was still holding it at a funny angle, and there were drops of blood where the brambles had cut it.

'I think I need to put you somewhere warm
and safe so you can heal.'

She dashed to the stables and came back a few
minutes later with a box. Gently she lifted the
owl in, resting him on a towel, and then carried
him back to the stables. Squill ran ahead, kicking
the low branches aside to clear a path. At the

stable door, he lifted both paws and gave a
puuuuuuush. It creaked open.

Tally blinked to adjust her eyes. There were
scratches and snuffles as the stable animals came
to greet her.

'Hello, Brie!' she said as the rat climbed on to her shoe. One of the rabbits nibbled at her laces.

She set the box down on the floor. Brie squeaked nervously and the rabbits moved back in fright.

'It's OK,' Tally said gently. 'I'll explain.' She looked at Mr Owl sternly. 'Here in the stables we have one important rule: friends don't eat friends.' Mr Owl ruffled his feathers in understanding.

'I'll get you a bit more straw,' said Tally. She moved to the back of the stable where there was a large pile of it. As she began to gather an armful, she noticed a dip in the straw, a hollowed-out section as if some small creature had made a nest there. Tally frowned. It wasn't the rabbits. They slept in a huddle under the woodpile. Tally had made them a bed there with soft wood shavings. Brie liked to sleep in the manor house. Tally reached down and pulled out a bit of grey fur that was caught in the hollow. Brie was white. The rabbits were black. Whose fur was this? She put

the grey fur in her petticoat pocket and turned
back to the owl.

'Don't try to fly till you're ready,' she advised
him. 'You need to get that wing better.'

The owl settled down in the straw, preening his
feathers[3] until he was comfortable.

Tally nodded. 'Right. Squill and I are
off to the Secret Library.' Squill puffed
himself up, trying to look important.
(The effect that was ruined by the
fact that he had bits of straw stuck
to his eyebrows.)

Tally stepped into the stone circle and the
air stilled.

There was a feeling here, a feeling of ancient
magic, of secrets and mysteries from long ago.
Tally went straight to the central stone, to the ten
holes carved into its old grey rock. This was the
key to the library, the coded puzzle that opened
the trapdoor. A cube had to be placed into each

---

[3] Birds use their beaks to preen their feathers, removing dust
and dirt. Preening keeps their feathers in good condition.

hole, in exactly the right arrangement. Each
cube had a symbol on it. Tally picked up the one
engraved with the outline of a hand. She began to
sing a song, a song Ma had taught her when she
was just a little girl.

'Give me your hand and we'll run
Down past the grass, up through the trees'

This song, together with a
tapestry hanging in the manor
house, helped her remember
how to order the cubes. She
put the hand cube into the
first hole. Squill solemnly
handed her the grass
one, then
the tree.

Give me your time and we'll sail
Down to the boat, up on the seas
Give me your heart and we'll fly
Up like a bee, down under leaves
This is the answer I know
This is the truth I will see.
This is the way I will go
Down where the gate waits for me.

Tally placed the last cube, the one with the gate symbol, into the bottom-right hole.

The ground shook and there was a loud creak as a hidden trapdoor in the grass slid back. By Tally's feet was a deep hole. She grinned at Squill. The entrance to the library was open!

Tally turned and gripped the rope ladder that dangled down from the top of the hole. Squill jumped over her and bounced down the rungs, balancing on just one paw at a time, as if to show off his skills.

'Yes, yes, I know how clever you are.' Tally smiled as she stepped into the hole, feeling for

each rung with her toes. Down and down she went, into the darkness, until she was deep under the manor grounds. Finally her foot landed on solid ground. Squill had already been from lamp to lamp, lighting each one so the library was bathed in soft light.

Tally took a breath. She loved it down here! No matter how many times Tally visited, she always felt a thrill run through her.

The Secret Library was no ordinary library. The books here were magical. Something very special happened every time Tally opened them here under the grounds of the manor house. The information within them had been gathered by monks hundreds of years ago, back when Mollett Manor was a monastery. It had been these monks who had hidden the library away, and coded the trapdoor. And the trapdoor wasn't the only puzzle at the manor. So far, Tally had also found:

two secret tunnels

a hidden cave

and a secret passage.

Mollett Manor was an unusual house – Tally had felt its magic the first moment she'd arrived all those years ago. Even as a little girl she'd sensed it. It was full of hidden secrets waiting to be discovered!

But of all of her discoveries, the Secret Library was her favourite. Tally loved books, and she loved finding things out. There were so many wonderful things to learn about the world! Because of the library, Tally now knew:

How to build a butterfly's chrysalis.[4] (This had come in very useful for storing Tally's precious things away from the eyes of Mrs Sneed. It clung to a dark corner above her sink bed in the scullery, holding her spider brooch every night while she slept.)

How to camouflage herself like an octopus.[5]

[4] A butterfly caterpillar builds a chrysalis, a moth caterpillar builds a cocoon.
[5] An octopus can change the colour of its skin almost instantly.

(She'd spent a whole hour blended into the wallpaper to avoid Mr Bood.)

How to roll into a ball, like a hedgehog.[6] (Squill and Tally had had a great time speed-rolling down the snowy manor hill.)

She'd saved the manor house from burglars using a spider's web, and even made a bloodhound's nose from a funnel and magical sniffing sense from Brie. It had been so amazing to smell all the different scents! The world was full of smells humans had no idea about. With the bloodhound nose, Tally had followed the popcorny scent of Widdles all the way to the village to save him from nasty Colin.

But she only had two years left to use the library. Tally was eleven years old and, as she knew:

[6] Hedgehogs have around 8,000 spines on their body. They roll into a ball to protect the softer parts of their body – the head, tail and legs.

The Secret Library's Rules:

There will be only one Secret Keeper
in each generation.

The Secret Keeper must be
under the age of thirteen.

The Keeper must guard the secret of
the library and the information within.

Talking is permitted.

For now, for the next two years, Tally was determined to visit the library as much as she could. She ran past the shelves of books, which twisted and turned up to the ceiling. She ran through the wonky aisles, passing:

HOW TO SHED SKIN by Anna Conda
WINTER HIBERNATION by Jan U. Airey
THE SECRETS OF FLIGHT by
Augusta Wind
NAVIGATING MIGRATION by Miles A. Way

She ran on, until she came to a pile of cushions on the floor. Squill was there already, plumping them up for her. This was their spot, and Tally kept a little box of biscuits and a glass bottle of water there ready for them.

'First we need to find out about the sleeping habits of dogs – for Lord Mollett,' she reminded Squill, and together they looked through the shelves. The books were very old, their covers

48

cracked from hundreds of years of use. Some of them were made from bamboo or silk. Some had even been bound with glue made from bluebells.[7]

'Ah!' Tally pulled down

HOW ANIMALS SLEEP by I. M. Tyred

and opened the book. All at once the lamps flickered. Tally grinned at Squill – she loved this bit! 'Here we go …' She began to read:

'Some animals sleep in the day and are active at night – they are nocturnal.'

And the magic began!

Holograms floated up just in front of Tally, looking as real as life. A sun shone down, filling the Secret Library with warmth and light. Tally jumped as a leopard appeared right by her toes, lazily snoozing in the hot sun. Squill stepped back nervously, just in case she woke up. There was a bat, and a badger and …

'Oh look, Squill! There are tawny owls here – just like our friend!'

---

[7] Bluebell glue was once used to hold pages together, and to attach feathers to arrows.

The owls were huddled together inside a hole in a tree.

'I wonder how they can sleep sitting up like that,' she said. 'Oh, it explains it here …'

'The "knees" of the owl point backwards, making a kind of platform. The feet lock into place, keeping the owl upright while it sleeps.'

Tally watched as the tawny owl settled down in the sunlight, resting his body on his backwards knees.

She turned the page and the images disappeared. Tally blinked, trying to readjust her eyes to the dim lamplight. She waited till her eyes were used to the light level, then read the next page out loud.

'*Some animals are most active at dawn and dusk – they are crepuscular,*' she read out. Images began to appear around her once again.

'Oh look – there's a gecko, just like our gecko!' It scuttled down the library wall. 'And a hamster! A little brown one!' Tally laughed at the hamster's fat cheeks. He was so cute! She turned the page.

'*Some animals sleep at night, and are active in the day – they are diurnal,*' she said out loud.

The library was suddenly plunged into darkness. As Tally's eyes adjusted, she could make out stars twinkling in the night sky and a soft yellow moon.

There before her was a dog, fast asleep and snoring. Tally could see his furry belly rising and falling and hear his soft breathing. To her left was a deer, curled up on the grass, and to her right, a gorilla, his arm tucked under his head.

Tally reached out to touch him, but her fingers slipped right through the moving image.

She closed the book and the holograms vanished.

'Well, now we've got our first fact for Lord Mollett: dogs are diurnal. So are you, Squill. I've heard you snoring next to me all night long.' Squill huffed and flicked his tail. Tally turned to the section called 'Dogs' to read more.

Before long she'd learned that:

Puppies need little naps during the day.

They like to curl up in a ball to keep themselves warm.

'And, Squill, it says here …' Tally put her finger on the line. '*Research suggests that dogs dream.*'

As she read the words, a hologram of a puppy rose up out of the book. It was curled up in a ball, fast asleep. Then it gave an excited little 'wuff' and its legs began to wriggle, moving in the air.

'I think he's dreaming about chasing sticks,' Tally said and Squill giggled as the puppy's feet twitched, '… or squirrels, maybe.'

Squill pushed the book closed hard, and the hologram vanished.

'All right,' Tally said. 'I think we have enough facts for Lord Mollett now. Let's read another couple of pages from Ma's diary.' Squill's ears pricked up.

Tally had found the diary last summer. It had been hidden in a little hole in the cliff edge. In it, Martha talked about her friend Bear – how much she loved him, how often they met to have picnics or walks. It hadn't taken long before Tally had realised that 'Bear' was Edward – Lord Edward Mollett. Martha and Edward had been in love. But then, something had happened. Some kind of scandal. And, by the time Tally was born, far away from the manor, Edward had no longer been a part of Ma's life. Tally was desperate to find out what had happened. Why had they stopped being friends? Why had Ma brought her back to the manor nine years ago? Down in the library was where Tally felt closest to Ma. She'd used this library too – she'd been a Secret Keeper, just like Tally.

She slid her fingers under the nearest shelf and pulled out a small leather-bound book. Tally was rationing it, only reading a bit at a time. This diary, and a scrap of lace from Ma's skirt, were all she had left of her mother. As much as she wanted to read every word of the diary – just gobble it up in one go – and as desperate as she was for facts about her past, Tally couldn't bear the thought of finishing, of no longer hearing Ma's voice in her head. She had decided that she was allowed to reread old pages whenever she liked, and she had read the pages about Edward over and over again. But she was only allowed to read new pages once a week. And only two at a time. She needed to make the diary last. It was too precious to use up all at once.

With trembling fingers, Tally opened the book. She fumbled for the bit of ribbon marking the page they were on. 'Are you ready?' she asked Squill. 'Perhaps we'll hear more about Ma's life –

about Edward or about my grandparents.' Tally's heart thudded with excitement. She stroked the

cover lovingly. When she'd first found the diary, she'd read its words *outside* the library and they'd just been, well, words. But *inside* the library … that was where the diary came to life, where she could see the moving image of Ma!

Tally couldn't wait to see her again. These little glimpses of her mother, even though they were wobbly and a bit see-through, were all she had. Tally's voice shook as she began to read:

'What shall I do? What will become of me?'

The hologram of Ma shimmered before her: she was seated at her desk, her dark curls jiggling as she wrote. But for once Ma didn't look happy. She was pale and worried. Her green eyes were narrowed. She chewed at her pencil. Her rabbit, Rabs, stroked her other hand and laid his cheek on her palm.

'Mother and Father will be so cross!' wrote Ma. 'And the Mollett family! They'll never accept it – not from a "village girl".'

A chill ran through Tally. What had happened? She read on as quickly as she could.

'But ... whatever they say ...' Ma looked up, then looked down and scribbled. 'I am happy.' In the diary, Tally could see the indentations, showing how firmly Ma had pressed down with her fountain pen. 'Happy' was underlined twice.

The hologram of Ma leaned back in her chair. She put her hand down to her tummy and rubbed it softly, lovingly, her palm moving round in a circle. Tally peered closely – Ma's tummy was bigger, fuller. It looked … it looked …

Tally dropped the book. The air in the library stilled. 'Ma is pregnant!'

Her breath caught. 'That's me,' she said. 'The baby. That's me.' In a daze she lifted the book and read on.

'I won't tell yet.' Ma's eyes were burning fiercely, her hologram lighting the library with its intensity.

'I won't tell anyone. It will be my secret.'

Tally closed the diary. She was shaking too much to read on. With trembling fingers, she folded the blanket, turned out the lamps and climbed up the ladder and out of the library.

She clenched her jaw tightly.

'Lord Mollett is my father,' she whispered to Squill, as she strode through the manor towards the kitchen. 'He is. Now I know for sure. I just have to prove it to him.' Squill jumped up on to her shoulder and bit one of her curls for good luck. 'But,' she whispered, 'will he even want me?'

It's for the best echoed in her head.

Squill stroked her head.

'Tally!' came Mrs Sneed's voice. 'Where are you, you lazy wretch?'

CHAPTER FOUR

'There you are!' Mrs Sneed harrumphed and cracked her spindly neck to the side.

Creaaak craaaack!

'I've been waiting for you for so long, I've even had time to finish three cups of tea!'

'Sorry,' said Tally.

'We're all very busy here!' Mrs Sneed insisted, as she adjusted the cushion behind her back to make the armchair more comfortable.

'Yes, Twooly.' Mr Bood nodded, wiping cake crumbs from his lap. 'Madame Sage is coming at seven o'clock this very evening, and there are lots of chores to do.'

'She's going to do *a science* in the ballroom!'

Mrs Sneed clapped her hands in excitement. Tally hadn't seen her quite so enthusiastic since the time the local village fete had run a cake-eating competition.

'It's called a *seance*, not a science,' Tally corrected her.

'Oh, seance, science; it's all the same thing, isn't it?' Mrs Sneed replied.

Not really, thought Tally.

'The ballroom floor is filthy,' said Mr Bood. 'It needs a thorough scrub.' He handed Tally a toothbrush.

'Tally – you are the *only* one who can do it …' said Mrs Sneed. Tally's eyebrows shot up. Was she about to get *praise*? '… because everyone else is dressed nicely,' she finished.

Mr Bood nodded and checked out his reflection in the cake knife – just in case Lady Beatrice urgently needed a model.

'You know, Squill,' grumbled Tally as she shuffled down the hall, Widdles snoozing on her feet, 'just because Mrs Sneed *looks* nasty and

spiky and grumpy, doesn't mean
she needs to *act* nasty and spiky
and grumpy.'

Squill stopped walking. He cocked
his head, waiting for something …

'EW!' came a cry from behind them,
back in the kitchen.

'Squill?' Tally looked at him. 'Did you put
salt in Mrs Sneed's cup of tea again?'

Squill looked sheepish (which is very difficult
for a squirrel) and Tally laughed.

Tally stopped just by the ballroom door.
On the wall hung a tapestry – Tally's favourite

one. It had been embroidered years ago, during the time Mollett Manor was a monastery. It was an idyllic scene, showing a group of monks standing in a garden. Bees buzzed around a hive behind the monks, and there was a boat in the foreground, sailing away on a river. Tally gave the tapestry a little stroke. The images were very special. Each image was carved into one of the cubes used to open the library trapdoor, and Ma's song mentioned every part of the tapestry.

'Ma,' whispered Tally. 'I miss you.' She touched one of the flowers and felt the bumpy silk threads. Squill stroked her neck with his tail. Widdles gave her ankle a lick.

'Come on.' She shook herself and opened the door to the ballroom, brandishing her toothbrush. She put her hands on her hips and assessed the room. This room of the house was hardly ever used. The Molletts hadn't had a single ball the whole time Tally had lived at the manor.

The chandelier hanging from the ceiling was sparkling, so that didn't need cleaning. The golden frames of the old paintings could do with a wipe, and some of the shiny ornaments on the shelves needed a polish. But the first job was the floor.

'You start at one end, Squill, and I'll start at the other.'

Squill swept across the ballroom with his tail, gathering the dust into a pile.

'Wuff! Wuff!' Widdles cried in joy. He leapt from Tally's feet and landed – *floof!* – in the dust.

'*Ahchoo!*' Squill sneezed as the dust flew up in the air.

'Ruff!'

Tally laughed at the squirrel's shocked little face. 'I'll open the window,' she said. 'We need some fresh air.' She pushed hard upwards on the old wooden sash. The window juddered open and she leaned out to breathe in the sharp, cold air. There were no footprints on the window sill but –

'What's this?' On the drainpipe just by the window was a little piece of fur, caught in the old metal. Tally yanked it free. It was grey. Tally

twisted her head, following
the drainpipe up with her
eyes. It ran all the way to
Lady Beatrice's bedroom.

'This is a clue, Squill!' said
Tally. 'I'm beginning to get
the feeling that I'm right –
it's not a ghost scaring Lady
Beatrice in the night, it's a
creature! A grey creature with
hand-like paws.' She pulled
the piece of grey fur from her
pinafore pocket to compare it
to the one from the drainpipe.
They matched. 'This is the
same fur as we saw in the
stables! But what creature is
it? And why is it visiting Lady
Beatrice's room?'

Just then, Lady Beatrice
appeared at the ballroom
door, holding her precious

camera. 'Oh dear!' she said when she saw Widdles. 'Lord William! You're filthy! Oh no! I wanted Madame Sage to see us looking elegant and smart and perfect. She could be our last hope, Tally, the only way to get rid of the ghost. We have to impress her – and now William is all grubby.'

'I'll give him a B-A-T-H right away.' Tally spelled the word because Widdles knew it and he didn't like baths.

Widdles woofed in excitement because he couldn't spell and thought he was going for a walk.

'B-A-T-H?' said Lady Beatrice, a wrinkle appearing between her eyebrows. 'B-A-T-H? Oh, bath. Yes, bath.'

'Ruff!' said Widdles in protest.

'No. Come on,' said Tally, scooping up the puppy as he tried to run away.

'What an excellent idea!' Lady Beatrice cheered up right away. 'Use my bath – it's the biggest. Can you curl his hair? And plait his whiskers?

And put ribbons on his tail? Tally, Tally …?'

Tally ran the water in the bath. She added Lady Beatrice's best bath cream and soon foam filled the marble tub.

'Right. In you go.' She lifted a wriggling Widdles into the water. 'Let's get that dust off.'

'Yip!' The puppy smacked his tail down crossly and water splashed everywhere. Squill jumped on to the golden taps, a scrubbing brush in his paws.

Tally held the puppy in place while Squill brushed every inch of dog fur. The dog was covered in soapy white bubbles.

Widdles wiggled and shook as Squill scrubbed him, sending foam flying across the bathroom.

'Keep still!' Tally told him. She lifted her head to avoid the splashing water and her eyes landed on the window. She hadn't checked this sill yet – and hadn't Lady Beatrice mentioned a tapping at her bathroom window? Tally stood up and pushed it open. There on the sill were the hand-like footprints.

'Oh!' she gasped. 'The creature came to this

window too, Squill. Another of Lady Beatrice's windows!'

In the bath, Widdles barked and bounced and suddenly …

'Stop him!' Tally cried, as the dog broke free and jumped out of the water. He ran across Lady Beatrice's bedroom leaving a trail of soap behind him. Squill dashed after him. The squirrel leapt on a high shelf and then dived down, landing straight on the puppy's back.

Tally ran after them. The squirrel was holding on tight to Widdles's diamond collar, his little red legs wrapped round the puppy's waist. Widdles barked and jumped, as Squill steered him at top speed around corners and down the stairs.

Along the tapestry corridor they galloped. Squill, holding himself close into Widdles's foamy fur, made a sharp turn into the ballroom by pulling on the dog's ear. 'Well done, Squill!' said Tally breathlessly. The ballroom was enormous. There was plenty of room for Widdles to run around in here.

The ballroom door opened and Mr Bood's fat head came into view.

'Twilly! What is all that noise?' He saw a long red tail twitching on top of a white fluffy mass.

'Eeek! A snake!' he cried. 'And it's riding a sheep!' He slammed the door closed and ran screaming down the corridor.

Widdles had stopped at the noise and now he gazed up at Tally in confusion.

'It's OK,' said Tally and she bent her head down to whisper: 'He's a very silly man.'

'Wuff!' agreed Widdles, chewing the end of Tally's boot.

By seven o'clock everything was ready.

The ballroom was clean and shiny.

Widdles was neat and brushed.

Mrs Sneed had eaten six extra biscuits, in preparation for the 'science'.

And Mr Bood had calmed down from seeing a vicious red snake. 'Really, Tooly, it was terrifying!'

There was a knock at the door and Lady Beatrice squealed, clutching her camera to her chest. Mr Bood opened the heavy front door, and there in the entrance stood a large woman. She wore a bright purple skirt and countless woollen scarves. In her hand was a wicker basket with a flip-top lid. She began to glide towards them, but the moment her toes touched the doorway, she stopped dead still, supported herself against the door frame, and gazed into the middle distance mysteriously.

Tally's heart thudded. Was this woman going to notice the magic of the manor house?

Madame Sage closed her eyes. 'Oooooh,' she moaned. 'I'm getting a sense ... a sense of ...' She opened her eyes abruptly. '... a ghost!'

Lady Beatrice shrieked and held her camera tight, just in case, at that very moment, a ghost decided to drop down and snatch it.

'Yes, my lady,' said Madame Sage seriously. 'I'm afraid you do have a ghost here.'

'Really?' said Tally. 'How do you know?'

Madame Sage bristled. She looked like a plump chicken shaking its feathers. 'I am in tune with …' She paused to gaze into the middle distance again. '… with the other.'

Widdles jumped up, sniffing at the basket in her hand.

'Lord William!' cried Lady Beatrice in horror. 'Oh, Madame Sage, I'm so sorry!'

Madame Sage lifted the basket high out of his reach. Tally pulled the puppy back but he strained at his collar, desperate for another sniff at the basket. Tally frowned and calmed him with a pat.

'We must begin our seance right away!' said Madame Sage. 'Here, servant, take my scarves.' Madame Sage put her basket down and began to unwind her many scarves. Layer by layer, off they came, from her shoulders into Tally's arms, until Tally was struggling to hold the bundle. Tally peered over the top of the pile. The apparently rotund Madame Sage had turned into a skinny beanpole.

Tally hung the coats and scarves on a coat rack. She picked up the basket. It was surprisingly heavy. What on earth was in there?

'No!' cried Madame Sage sharply. She yanked the basket back. 'I will carry my own things,' she said firmly, as she flounced off after Mr Bood. The rest of the group followed.

Lord Mollett looked back at Tally and winked kindly. But Tally was distracted – there was a little piece of straw on the sole of Madame Sage's shoe. Tally could see it every time the medium lifted her foot.

Madame Sage sat at the table which had been set up in the ballroom. Her sharp eyes flicked around the room, taking in all the fine ornaments and paintings, and finally alighting on Lady Beatrice's prized camera.

'I certainly think this may take more than one visit,' she said with a teeny smile.

'Why's that?' Tally responded, sitting down next to her.

'Well, there's such a lot of … aura,' said Madame Sage. 'Now, before I begin there's just the small matter of' – she coughed – 'my recompense.'

'Recompense?' Lady Beatrice said, looking blank.

'She wants you to pay her,' Tally whispered to Lady Beatrice.

'Oh, "pay" is such an ugly word,' said Madame Sage. 'I just can't seem to sense the ghosts unless I am fairly rewarded,' she explained.

Lady Beatrice took out her purse and filled Madame Sage's open hand with coins.

'The spirits know all,' said Madame Sage, opening the other hand. 'They don't come if they feel I haven't been fully appreciated.'

Lady Beatrice filled the other hand with coins too.

Tally clenched her teeth. Lord Mollett was frowning too.

'Now, close your eyes,' Madame Sage told everyone. 'I need to get a feel for this house before the seance begins.'

Everyone obeyed, but Tally peeked a teeny bit. She saw Madame Sage looking down at her lap. On her knees were scrunched-up pieces of paper.

'I'm getting a sense … from the past … a sense of trouble,' breathed Madame Sage. 'Confusion … upset … scandal … a broken promise.' She said the last word more sharply and Lady Beatrice jumped. 'Oh, the spirits tell me … what's that? Something happened here twelve years ago. Something that caused a disturbance.'

Tally peeped again to see Lord Mollett turn pale.

'Oh yes,' continued Madame Sage in her floaty way. 'The vibrations are very strong here, I'm sensing …'

Tally felt something soft brush her leg. She opened her eyes. Squill was creeping towards Madame Sage's basket! Closer and closer … his

paw tried to lift the lid but it was too tight for
his little claws. Tally inched her toe towards the
lid to help him. All of a sudden, Madame Sage
opened her eyes and glared at Tally. She swooped
down and smacked Tally's hand on to the top of
the basket. Tally yanked her foot back as Squill
jumped clear.

'Stop!' cried Madame Sage. Four pairs of eyes
shot open. 'There are negative forces in our
presence. A cynic.' Madame Sage glared at Tally.

'I can't possibly continue today. Not with this
child present. Which is a great shame because I
haven't made as much progress as I'd hoped,' she

continued, tucking away the purse where she had put Lady Beatrice's money.

'I will return tomorrow at midnight, and we will start the seance – with grown-ups only.'

With that, she picked up her basket and flounced out of the ballroom. Everyone sat in shock. They heard her heels tap, tap, tapping away down the hall. The noise stopped. Tally listened: there was a creak, a rustle and a snap. Then Madame Sage tap, tap, tapped back to the ballroom again.

'The spirits are very upset.' She closed her eyes and pinched the bridge of her nose. 'Don't be surprised if they are cross in the night.'

Lady Beatrice gasped at that.

'And,' said Madame Sage with a stern look, 'we are going to need a lot more coins to appease them tomorrow night.'

Everyone followed her back out into the hallway where Tally handed her the scarves one by one. She lifted the basket to give it back and stifled a cry of surprise. The basket was so light.

It's empty! Tally realised.

Madame Sage glared at Tally in fury and snatched the basket back.

Then she was gone.

CHAPTER FIVE

Tally was in disgrace.

'You spoiled the seance.' Mr Bood breathed in sharply, his huge tummy filling with air. For a moment he looked like an enormous balloon.

'Science,' corrected Mrs Sneed, as she gave Tally her spikiest look.

'Tally – perhaps it *is* better if you don't come tomorrow night,' said Lady Beatrice, pulling Widdles on to her lap.

Even Lord Mollett was frowning. 'It's for the best,' he said, resting his hand on Tally's shoulder.

Tally swallowed.

Her senses were hyper-aware. She could feel

the air heavy around her as she turned. She walked away from the group, down the hallway towards the kitchen. Every step she took sounded loud in her ears. She didn't breathe until she entered the scullery.

She slumped against the wall by her sink-bed. She felt all alone. Why did everyone believe that woman? Madame Sage was clearly a fraud. Why couldn't they see it? She pictured Lord Mollett's face, a frown between his eyebrows. He'd looked … disappointed. He'd looked like she'd let him down. *It's for the best.*

Tally closed her eyes. *He doesn't want me for a daughter. What if, when I prove it, he throws me out?* A tear trickled down her face.

All at once a burst of red fur shot out of her pinafore pocket and sprang up on to her shoulder. A little paw wiped her tears away, and the warm soft bundle snuggled into Tally's neck.

'Thanks, Squill,' she whispered, and the girl and squirrel stood there, leaning into each other.

Squill gave a little chatter. He dived back down

into her pinafore pocket and popped out again. This time he was clutching some scrunched-up pieces of paper in his paws.

'Squill! Did you take those from Madame Sage?' Tally took them from his paws. 'That's a bit naughty … but at least now we can see what Madame Sage was reading during the seance! I just know that woman is up to no good.'

The papers were newspaper cuttings from *The Ton Express*. Tally spread them out on the kitchen table. They were about the Mollett family!

<u>ELIGIBLE</u>
Lord Mollett appeared the very picture of an English gentleman at last night's ball to celebrate the engagement of his sister, Beatrice, to the noble Duke of Swantingdon. The Lord danced with Baroness Greenbrough-Snuff and the Duchess of Wigglecoombe. What's stopping this eligible bachelor from taking the plunge with one of these fine aristocratic ladies?

Lady Beatrice engaged? thought Tally. And a ball at Mollett Manor as well. 'That's strange, isn't it Squill?'

Tally read on to the next paragraph.

NO GENTLEMAN

Well, *The Ton Express* can exclusively reveal exactly what is making Lord Mollett so reluctant to marry. Our sources tell us that last week the hesitant grandee was spotted wandering in the woods with a village girl! It seems Edward Mollett is no gentleman!

'*Village girl,*' Tally read out loud. Where had she heard that before? Of course, in Ma's diary. That's what Ma said they were calling her. 'Squill, the newspaper is talking about Lord Mollett and Ma!'

Tally turned to the next piece of paper, dated a few days later.

BROKEN OFF!

The Duke of Swantingdon has broken off his engagement to Lady Beatrice Mollett, sister of the disgraced Lord Edward Mollett. We at *The Ton Express* entirely support his decision.

NO MORE PARTIES

After the scandal of her brother and the village girl exposed by our own reporters last week, what did the Molletts expect? The once gay manor will be a lonely place for some time to come.

'Poor Lady Beatrice. No wonder she's been hiding herself away in the manor all these years. This article explains the reason hardly anyone comes to visit. How awful!'

Tally put down the papers. 'And do you know what else, Squill? Madame Sage is a fake,' she declared. 'The spirits didn't tell her all this information – she read it in a newspaper. But what I really want to know is: what was in that basket? It was heavy when she arrived but light when she went. What was it she left here at the manor? And why?'

Mrs Sneed burst into the kitchen with stomping feet, and Tally rushed to hide the newspapers in her pinafore pocket.

'Well, I hope you're happy,' she exclaimed. 'Actually. No … I hope you're not happy – don't I?' she added with a confused wave of her arms, completely missing the point of sarcasm.

Tally silently handed her a cup of tea.

'Humph.' Mrs Sneed plonked herself down in the armchair.

Tally silently handed her a biscuit.

'Humph.' There was a crunch as Mrs Sneed tucked in.

Tally dried the last of the dishes. She was itching to ask Mrs Sneed something. She waited until the third cup of tea (and the fifth cherry biscuit).

'What was the scandal Madame Sage talked about?' she asked gently.

'Humph. Well …' Mrs Sneed looked trapped

between her reluctance to give Tally the information she wanted and her desire to gossip.

Tally helped Mrs Sneed adjust the cushion behind her back to offer some encouragement. 'Something about a broken promise …?'

'Well, I suppose it's all history now.' Mrs Sneed's voice softened. 'Lady Beatrice was engaged once, and she was so happy. Although, her fiancé was a right bossy boots. Kept telling everyone how lucky her ladyship was to have him. If you ask me, it was the other way round.' Mrs Sneed sniffed. 'What was his name, the Duke of Swing … er … Swangdong … Swattytown.'

'Swantingdon,' Tally interjected.

'That's the chap. Anyway, Lord Mollett seemed very happy too – he'd been dancing around the manor for months, singing songs and smiling all day. Turns out he was in love as well. But not with any of those society ladies like Baroness … err …'

'Greenbrough-Snuff,' Tally suggested.

'Yes, her, or the Duchess of Whachamacallit.'

'Wigglecoombe?'

'That's right.' Mrs Sneed paused and looked at Tally with a puzzled expression. 'Well, anyway. It wasn't any of that lot. Someone spotted him walking out with a village girl! It was in the papers. It was a big scandal.'

'Why?'

'Well. Lords are supposed to marry ladies. The world is funny that way.' Mrs Sneed waved her hand dismissively. 'And they were unchaperoned, you see. No adult or friend was with them. That was the worst of it. Men and women shouldn't really be on their own until they are betrothed.'

Tally frowned.

'It's silly, I know,' said Mrs Sneed. 'We could all see how happy that village girl made his lordship.' She leaned forward in her chair. 'The day after it was reported in the paper, a letter arrived for Lady Beatrice. It was from the duke. He broke off the engagement. Said Lady Beatrice wasn't a proper kind of lady – that the Molletts weren't the right kind of family.'

Mrs Sneed looked really angry in a way Tally had never seen before. It wasn't her usual irritability, but a type of angry that comes from deep down inside.

Tally clenched her fist. This must why Lady Beatrice read MRS PRIMM'S GUIDE TO BEING A LADY over and over again. Because of something that silly duke had said.

'Lady Beatrice is proper. This *is* the right kind of family,' said Tally fiercely.

'I know, dear,' said Mrs Sneed, absent-mindedly.

Dear? Dear?

Mrs Sneed had never called Tally anything nice her entire life!

'Well, we were none of us quite ourselves after that. Lord Mollett was sorry of course, but he said he didn't regret what he had done. He really loved that village girl. Said he wanted to marry her.'

Tally's heart soared. 'What was her name? What happened next?' she blurted out.

'Oh, I don't know her name. She just disappeared. Went away. Lord Mollett didn't know why. Broke his heart, she did.' Mrs Sneed stood up. She cracked her neck. 'And he's never seen her since.'

Tally was shaking with excitement. She knew what she was going to do. She was going to break one of her own rules. She waited till Mrs Sneed had gone to bed.

'Come on, Squill,' she whispered. 'We're going to the Secret Library. I have to read more of Ma's diary.'

Tally darted to the fireplace in the scullery. Over the mantelpiece was carved:

Tally knew that rearranged this spelled:

PRESS X TO OPEN

She pressed the X and the stone fireplace slid away to reveal a dark passage. Tally and Squill hurried down it as fast as they could. Tally held her lamp high as they ran under the manor and up to the secret door of the infirmary, the old monks' hospital. Through the ward they ran, then out past the malthouse to the stone circle. Tally fumbled with the cubes,

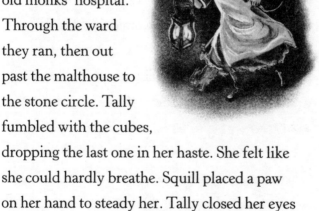

dropping the last one in her haste. She felt like she could hardly breathe. Squill placed a paw on her hand to steady her. Tally closed her eyes for a moment. She breathed in slowly. Then she picked up the cube marked with the gate and put it in the final hole.

It wasn't long before they were underground,

in the Secret Library, sitting on their old blanket.
Tally had the diary in her hands. 'OK, Squill,'
she said in a whisper. 'Let's find out for ourselves
what happened next.' Tally opened the book
where they had left off and turned the page.
Here Ma's writing was messy and jumbled. Her
words were hard to read. It looked like she had
scribbled everything at top speed. Tally tilted her
head to try to make the letters out. She began to
read aloud:

'They know!! Everyone knows about Edward
and me.' The hologram of Ma burst out of the
book. Her face was white against the yellow bird
wallpaper in her bedroom. 'I've had to tell Mother
and Father my big secret too and they are so cross.
I've never seen Pa this angry.' Tally bit her lip.
'They are making me go away. They won't let me see
Bear! I have to leave first thing in the morning. They
want to go somewhere no one knows us.' Ma gave a
sob. 'Oh, my poor Bear!'

This bit of the diary was smudged and blotted

with tears. It was hard to read what Ma had
written.

'I won't leave him without a word. I can't. I'll write
him a letter. I can climb up the tree by his room – I've
done it before. Then I'll hide this diary somewhere
it'll be safe from them – somewhere only I know. One
day I'll come back.' The hologram of Ma touched
her belly. 'I'll come back and I'll find Edward.'

Tally turned the page as fast as she could.
There was only one more entry – messy and
scribbled, as though Ma had written it at great
speed. Tally's voice trembled as she read the final
words.

'I left Bear the letter.'

Hologram Ma rose up in the library. An image
of the moon shone bright, sending soft white
light across the library floor. Tally gasped.

'Ma is standing on the cliffs at Mollett Manor!'

She stared at her mother. This would be her
last glimpse of her, and Tally couldn't take her
eyes off Ma's familiar face, her soft curls and her
gentle hands.

'Mummy,' she whispered, as she watched Ma
write the final entry. But of course, hologram Ma
couldn't hear her.

'Just as I dropped it into his window, someone
appeared and I had to rush away or risk being
caught!'

The scene transformed. Now the hologram
showed a dark room. Tally squinted. She could
hardly see anything.

'I think that's Lord Mollett's bedroom,' she said, screwing up her eyes to make it out.

The bedroom door opened and a dim shaft of light appeared from the hallway. A figure walked towards Tally. It looked like a woman, but the light was behind her so Tally couldn't see who it was. The figure bent down and picked something up.

'Ma's letter!'

The hologram wobbled and the scene changed back again. There was Ma at the cliff edge, the very edge she was to fall over two years later. She scribbled the last words in the diary.

'He'll wait for me once he reads it. He'll wait.'

Ma closed the diary. As the hologram faded Tally could just make out Ma reaching down to hide it in a hole in the cliff – and then the hologram disappeared.

CHAPTER SIX

Widdles was taking up all the room in her sink-bed, forcing Tally's toes to cramp up under the tap.

Thoughts were spinning around Tally's head: the footprints, the fur, the straw on Madame Sage's foot, the empty basket, all those coins clinking into the medium's hands.

On top of all that, she couldn't stop thinking about Ma and Lord Mollett. The diary had told her there had been a letter from Ma. A letter Lord Mollett had never seen. Surely, he hadn't? If he had, he'd know there was child out there: his child … unless … he had seen it and … and …

It's for the best.

Tally pulled the thin blanket up over her shoulder.

Where was the letter? Who was the woman who'd picked it up off the bedroom floor? Was it Mrs Sneed? Tally stilled. Mrs Sneed couldn't read. She'd never been able to. She always got Tally to read the local newspaper out loud to her. To the housekeeper, that letter would have just been squiggles. If she'd found it, she might have thrown it away!

Tally ground her teeth in frustration. Widdles rolled on to his back, his puppy feet scrabbling in the air as he dreamed about chasing sticks, just like the puppy in the hologram.

It was no use. Even though it was the middle of the night, Tally couldn't sleep. She had to do *something*.

She climbed out of her sink. Sleepily, Squill clambered into her pinafore pocket and curled up at the bottom. *I'll make Lord Mollett's favourite biscuits,* she decided. *That will calm me down.*

Tally lit the kitchen lamp. She glanced up at

the old recipe, stuck to the kitchen wall. It was
a bit faded now, and the edges were curling
away from the wall. She put her fingers into the
butter and flour, squishing them together. She
felt more peaceful
already, the familiar
activity soothing her
busy brain. Squill
snored softly from
her pocket and Tally
smiled. Peace at last.
A soft hoot came from
outside and Tally turned her head to
the kitchen window. There, silhouetted against
the moon, was the tawny owl. Tally smiled – he
was well enough to fly again! He dipped his wing
at her in greeting then flew off to hunt, his eyes
sharp enough to see in the dark. Squill squeaked
in his sleep.

Just as Tally was measuring out the icing sugar,
she heard a strange noise. It was a low, groaning
kind of noise. She wiped her hands and made her

way into the hallway. There she stood stock still and listened again.

Grooooooo went the noise. Tally frowned. It was coming from the blue drawing room.

Tally looked at the clock in the hall – midnight. *No one should be up at this hour. And certainly not in the drawing room.* She stepped out of the kitchen, and silently on to the first stair. She made her way up as carefully as possible, feeling her way in the dim light and staying off the creaky bit on the tenth stair.

On the landing, she put her fingers on the door handle. She could feel Squill tense in her pinafore pocket. Tally told a deep breath and quickly pushed down the handle, shoving the door open hard. 'Hello?' she called. The room was grey and dim – and empty. Tally shivered. **Grooooooo**.

This time the noise came from the other end of the house.

Squill jumped straight out of her pocket in fright. And then straight back in again for safety. For a moment Tally froze, then she ran down the corridor, following the sound. Here at the east wing were doors to three bedrooms – Lord Mollett's, Lady Beatrice's and the red bedroom.

Just as she opened the red bedroom door, there was a *whooooosh!* Something brushed past her ankle, tickling the bottom of her leg. Tally fumbled with the lamps, but by the time she had them lit, the something was gone. A chill ran over her. Could … could it be a ghost?

Grooooooooo came the noise, from back in the blue drawing room.

Tally whirled around. There's no such thing as ghosts, she told herself. No such thing.

'Right, Squill,' she whispered out loud. 'Something is making that sound – and we're going to catch it!'

Squill waved his paw as if to say, *How?* But

Tally had a plan. The something was running back and forth between the east and west wings, groaning at one end of the house, and then the other. It moved so fast they'd never catch it in the corridor. But Tally knew a secret passage, one that ran east to west, between the red bedroom and the blue drawing room. If they could sneak up on the something, then they could ambush it!

Tally ran straight to the fireplace in the red bedroom. On the wall above it was a puzzle.

It was a series of numbers. They needed to be rearranged so that every row and every column added up to fifteen. Tally pulled out the wooden blocks as quickly as she could. She moved them around until she had:

A door inside the fireplace clicked open, and Tally slipped behind it. She felt her way down the dark passageway, her hands on either side of the stone walls, until she came to a door at the other end.

'We're here,' she whispered. 'We're in the west wing, behind the fireplace of the blue drawing room.'

Silently they waited. They heard the **Grooooooo** from the east wing of the house.

'It will be coming back here next,' Tally whispered to Squill.

Sure enough, before long there was a scuffling sound.

Tally sprang out from the fireplace and pulled back the curtain. A beam of moonlight lit the room. In the pale light Tally saw a tiny grey thing with a long tail and two enormous eyes. Then it was gone, darting out of the room and down the stairs. Tally rushed to the top of the stairs just in time to see it leap out of the hallway window and into the snowy night.

'Tally!' came a scream from Lady Beatrice's room. 'Help!'

'There, there.' Tally was patting Lady Beatrice's shoulder. Even after three cups of tea, Lady Beatrice was still trembling. Lord Mollett stood by the fireplace in his bunny-print pyjamas, looking thoughtful.

'It's ghosts!' Lady Beatrice cried, over and over.

'Madame Sage said the spirits would be back.'
She clutched her handkerchief. 'Now there are
two of them groaning. I heard them at both ends
of the house. Oh, I'm going to give that woman
whatever it takes to get rid of them.'

'It wasn't ghosts,' Tally said for the tenth time.

'Oh, you know nothing, Tally!' Lady Beatrice
snapped. She held her camera so tightly her
knuckles turned white. 'And you are not allowed
at the seance tonight!'

'Now, now, Beatrice,' said Lord Mollett. 'Come
on, Tally, let's give my sister a bit of time to rest.'

He led Tally out of the room and into the
corridor.

'I'm sorry my sister was so abrupt with you,'
he said. 'Beatrice is such a delicate soul, and she's
been so upset recently. It's such a shame. She was
doing so well.' He stopped at *Widdles Confused
by Snow*. 'And her photographs are jolly clever.
I do hope this Madame Sage can sort everything
out.'

Tally clenched her teeth. Even Lord Mollett
was fooled. It made her more determined than

ever to find out what Madame Sage was up to. She looked down and fiddled with the spider brooch, pinned to her pinafore. Lord Mollett had given it to her last year, after she'd saved the manor from burglars. He'd told her that someone special had made it for him. Tally stroked the centrepiece, made from pale green sea glass. Lord Mollett's eyes followed her fingers.

'That brooch is all I had left of her,' he said.

Tally tensed. 'Who?' she asked, trying to hide the tremble in her voice.

'Twelve years ago I fell in love with the most wonderful person. She was clever like you.' Lord Mollett gave a sad smile. 'But then she left me.'

'What was her name?' Tally hardly dared breathe.

'Martha,' said Lord Mollett dreamily. 'I still think of her every day.'

'Edward!' called Lady Beatrice. 'Edward!'

Tally couldn't go back to sleep. Even though it

was the middle of the night, all she could think about was Ma. Lord Mollett still loved Martha! She had to find that letter. It could have clues to where Ma had gone. And it would tell Lord Mollett about the baby. His baby. Tally. A fragile feeling of hope rose inside her.

If he still loves Ma, maybe he'll love me too?

On top of that, there was the 'ghost'. The thing Tally had seen definitely wasn't a ghost. It was a small animal, furry and grey. The same colour as the fur on the drainpipe, and in the stable straw.

'Oh, I wish we had managed to see inside Madame Sage's basket, Squill. Widdles sniffed and sniffed at it. I'm sure there was something in there – and I think it was the creature we saw!'

Squill's bushy eyebrows shot up.

'I think Madame Sage let him out of the basket to cause mischief. That's why the basket was empty when I lifted it the second time. We need to watch that seance, Squill, to keep an eye on Madame Sage.'

While everyone slept, Tally crept into the ballroom. 'If they won't allow me to go, I'll have to find a way to watch without anyone knowing I'm there.'

The curtains weren't long enough to hide behind. Under the table was no good either – they'd see her when they came in.

'I wonder,' said Tally, spinning slowly in place. She was looking for secret passages. She checked the fireplace – nothing there. She checked the window bay – nothing in the panels there. Could there be a trapdoor? She bent down and squinted at the marble floor, but there wasn't anything odd or unusual.

Tally crossed to the other side of the room and ran her fingers over the wall panelling. There was a faint crack here in one of the panels, a long line running vertically down like a soft groove in the wood. Tally pressed the panel, but nothing happened. Then she looked up – there in the corner of the panel, was a tiny dial. It was exactly the same colour as the panel, hidden in a knot of the old wood. Tally turned it and it clicked softly with every turn. Still nothing happened.

'It's a combination lock,' said Tally.

Then Tally noticed something: to the left of the dial were symbols. It was another puzzle! It looked like this:

'We have to work out the value of each symbol,' said Tally. 'Three stars make three, so …' She looked at Squill. He just stared back blankly. 'Each star must be worth one.'

She worked through the puzzle:

'Two hearts and a star make seven. If the star

is worth one, then the two hearts together must be worth six. Which means one heart must be worth three.'

She put her finger on the final part.

'Star plus heart plus moon equals eight. So that's one plus three plus something equals eight … oh, the moon must be four!'

She looked at Squill. *Now what?*

CHAPTER SEVEN

Tally looked at the dial.

She now had three numbers: one, three and four. Was she supposed to add them up? Tally added up 1 + 3 + 4 and tried turning the dial right for 8 clicks. Nothing.

She tried turning it left for 8 clicks. Nothing.

She looked at the puzzle again. The middle line was further right than the other two. Did that mean something? Was it a clue?

She glanced at the ballroom door hoping no one was coming, then with trembling fingers Tally turned the dial left for one click, right for three clicks. She held her breath, then turned the dial left for four clicks.

There was a whirr, the sound of an old mechanism clicking into place. Tally grinned at Squill. It had worked.

The wood creaked and a door in the panelling swung open to reveal a small cupboard. A secret hidey-hole! It wasn't very big – it had probably been used to hide treasure. But it was big enough for a girl and a squirrel.

They had found their hiding place for the seance.

Tally and Squill snuggled up close on their blanket. It was chilly down here in the library early in the morning. But there was so much work to do. Madame Sage was coming back that night.

'Let's examine the facts, Squill.' Tally counted them off on her fingers.

'One: we found footprints on the window sills outside Lady Beatrice's rooms – and her rooms only.

Two: we found grey fur on the drainpipe and in

the straw inside the stable.

Three: Madame Sage had a basket that smelled funny. It was empty after she'd visited us.

Four: Madame Sage had straw on her shoe.

Five: Madame Sage had newspaper cuttings all about Lady Beatrice's past.

Six: we saw a creature last night. A creature that would fit in a basket. It is agile enough to climb, it has grey fur and it has hand-like paw prints.'

Squill yawned sleepily.

'You're making me yawn too,'[8] said Tally. She stretched. 'It's because we're diurnal, Squill. We should sleep at night, but we've spent all night running around after that creature.' Tally sat up straight. 'Wait a minute!'

She pulled down **HOW ANIMALS SLEEP by I.M. Tyred** and turned to the list of nocturnal animals.

'The library already showed us a leopard, a bat, a badger and an owl, but I wonder …'

---

[8] Yawns can be contagious. Around half of humans yawn when another person yawns. But scientists still can't agree on why.

Tally scanned the page, looking for the names of other nocturnal animals.

'Oh!' she said and read the next bit out loud: '*Opossums are nocturnal.*'

A hologram rose up. It showed a small, grey animal with a white face and round black ears. It had a little pink nose. Its paws had four long fingers and a thumb. In the darkness of the library it scuttled, low to the ground, and Tally could hear the *click-clack* of its claws on the stone floor.

'That's it,' cried Tally.

'That's the creature we saw last night!' She looked back down at the book. '*Opossums are excellent climbers.*'

The hologram flickered. A mighty tree grew up out of library floor, towering above Tally. The opossum grasped a low hanging branch with his hand-like paw and swung himself up. His tail curled round the next branch up, and he pulled himself high into the air.

'*The opossum has a prehensile tail,*' read Tally. 'That means he can hold things with it, and swing from it.' Squill looked a bit jealous and Tally gave him a sympathetic look. 'You have a great tail, Squill. You might not be able to swing from it, but it does help you balance. And it's wonderfully warm to snuggle up to at night.' Squill shrugged, but Tally could tell he was pleased.

She closed the book and began to pace around the library. 'Now why would Madame Sage want an opossum? She's trained it, it seems. But why choose an opossum? Why not a monkey or a squirrel?'

Squill nodded wisely as if to say, *Of course squirrels are the obvious choice for everything!*

'Why might she need a nocturnal animal?' Tally thought about what she'd learned. She pictured her friend the owl, flying in the moonlight. Nocturnal creatures were used to the dark. They hunted in the dark, foraged in the dark, because, because …

'Because they can see in the dark!' Tally said

in triumph. 'Madame Sage wants a creature that can see in the dark, a nocturnal creature that can scare Lady Beatrice at night. An opossum! And,' Tally added, 'she wants the seance at midnight, when the opossum is wide awake, so she can use him to trick Lady Beatrice out of even more money. Oooh, that woman! She's a con artist and a thief!'

Tally turned slowly on her heel, looking round the library. 'We already have a place to hide,' she said. 'But we can't catch the opossum tricking us if we can't see it. We need to be able to see in the dark as well, just like nocturnal animals do. Then we'll catch them red-handed.'

Squill examined his paws, confused.

'It's just an expression, Squill,' Tally explained. 'It means we'll catch them in the act.'

Tally ran her fingers along the books, walking slowly up and down the aisles. Her eyes caught a little glow from the bottom shelf. She crouched down and pulled out a slim black book. It felt strangely heavy in her hands. She turned it to read the cover.

NIGHT VISION by Seymour Starz

The words were scratched into the cover,
almost invisible. It looked as if the whole book
were filled with darkness. Tally breathed in
slowly. Squill flicked his tail. Together they took
the book back to the blanket and Tally opened
the stiff cover. The pages were bound fast
together, locked in place. Inside the cover were
the words:

This book will tell you how to see in the dark.
But you must promise never to give the
secret away.

Tally held Squill's paw as she
whispered the magic words:

'I promise.'

The library lamps flickered
and the book gave a little
sigh. It fell open,
releasing the pages.

The paper inside was black and a mist rose up,
curling into the still library air. Tally read from
the silver writing:

'The eyes of nocturnal animals are specially

115

adapted to see in the dark.'

A giant eye rose up in front of Tally. She leaned in to see. The black of the eye, the pupil, was much bigger than her own pupils – it filled nearly the whole of the coloured area of the eye.[9]

'All eyes have a retina, a lining in the eye, which contains "rods" and "cones". Rods are to see in dim light, and cones are to see colours.'

The eye turned to the side to show a cross section:

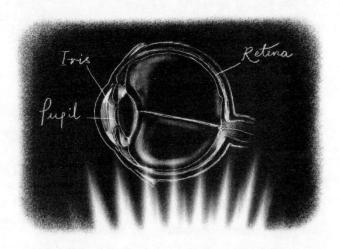

[9] If humans had the same eye to brain ratio as the tarsier (a nocturnal animal), our eyes would be the size of grapefruits.

'Nocturnal animals have more rods in their retina, helping them to see better in dim light.'

The hologram zoomed in now, showing Tally the area of the retina in more detail.

'Behind the retina is a special layer, with a surface of crystals. It is called the "bright carpet".[10] *Light hits the crystals and bounces off again, giving the animal's eye two chances to see an object.'*

Tally turned the page and the eye disappeared. The title of the next page was 'How to See in the Dark'.

Tally read through the equipment they would need, nodding her head as she worked out where to find each item.

She grinned at Squill. Now they would have their hiding place *and* their night vision!

The malthouse was full of old junk. In the olden days, it had been a building where the monks used to make ale. Nowadays it was filled with anything Mr Bood couldn't be bothered to fix

[10] Its Latin name is *tapetum lucidum*.

117

(which was a lot of things).

Tally pictured the diagram in the book's instructions.

'First we need mirrors, Squill.' Tally rummaged through the mass of broken lawnmowers, bits of piping, a clock that no longer worked and rusty garden tools. Squill dived in too, sniffing out exactly what they needed. Moments later, he popped up again from a pile of wood, a triumphant grin on his face.

'Nice!' cried Tally. The mirror Squill held up was broken, and Tally laid each piece out on the floor of the malthouse.

'Hmmm, now where did I see those bits of old pipe?'

Bit by bit, Tally and Squill constructed their night goggles. Soon they had two short metal tubes, with a series of mirrors stuck inside, each one at a different angle.

'Now we need the lenses from some old glasses,' said Tally, her eyes narrowing as she looked round the dusty room.

'Aha!' Over there was a chest marked in Lady Beatrice's handwriting:

Unfashnibble Things

This was full to the brim with items that Lady Beatrice used to wear but had stopped the moment MRS PRIMM'S GUIDE TO BEING A LADY (her favourite fashion guide) had told her not to.

There were hats, scarves and, yes! Pairs of spectacles.

Tally pulled off the lenses from two pairs and stuck them at the front and end of her night goggles.

The final ingredient Tally needed was:

Essence of Sight.

This was the magical, extra ingredient she needed to make the night goggles. It had to come from a creature that could see in the dark and, as the magic book told her:

'The essence must be granted willingly.'

Tally looked up at Squill. She knew exactly who to ask.

Tally carefully picked her way across the dark wood. The forest floor was uneven, covered with fallen branches and stones.

'Whoops!' she cried, tripped over yet another bump. She peered into the trees, straining her eyes to see.

'Mr Owl?' she called up. 'Are you here?'

There was a rustle from the branch above, and in the dim light Tally caught sight of the owl's brown speckled wings. His injured wing looked much better now. Squill chattered nervously and burrowed down in her pinafore pocket.

Tally set a saucer on the snowy ground.

The library had taught her the magic words to say – words she had used to ask spiders for the secrets of cobwebs, and Brie for her powerful sense of smell.

She closed her eyes and, in a clear voice, said:

'Owl, Owl
My heart is true
Help me learn
To do what you do.'

She stood back and waited behind a tree. There was a gust of air, and the huge owl swooped down. He bent over the saucer and blinked, then flapped his wings and flew back up into the tree.

Tally stepped forward slowly. There in the saucer was a shiny black gel. Tally touched it and it rippled in the moonlight. Her own face looked back at her, curls peeping out from under a cap.

'Thank you,' she called to the owl, as she dipped her fingers into the gel and smeared it on to the lenses of her goggles. Then, she paused.

On her knees, she stared at the forest around her. It was dark, the moonlight shielded by dense branches. Tally could hear the scuffle and rustle of animals moving, but in the blackness her eyes couldn't make out any shapes. She gripped her new device more tightly.

'Here we go, Squill,' she said. 'Let's see if these work.'

She lifted the night goggles to her face and fastened the leather cord around the back of her head.

Tally closed her eyes for a moment and when she opened them again, it was as if she could see another world before her! She gasped. The forest was teeming with animals – animals that slept in the day and only came out at night. Little grey moths flittered from plant to plant, dancing and circling one another. A badger[11] poked the snow with his nose, looking for worms or grubs to eat. His black and white head bobbed up and down, clear and bright even in the night.

A branch cracked behind her and Tally whipped her head around. There stood a fox,

[11] Some animals hibernate in the winter, which means they slow their bodies right down – almost like sleeping. Hedgehogs can slow their heartrate from 190 beats per minutes to 20 beats. Badgers do not hibernate; they are active all year round.

elegant and proud. He
stared right at her.
From her crouched
position, the fox looked
enormous, a fierce
hunter, with sharp
teeth and bright eyes.
He pricked his ears to

listen, then wiggled his bottom. Tally's
heart pounded as she watched him leap into the
air and pounce, landing right on the snow and
pulling out a sleeping wood mouse.[12]

'Let's go, Squill,' whispered Tally urgently.
'We really don't want to watch him eat that
mouse.'

She sprang to her feet and ran out of the
forest. With the night goggles she could see the
ground clearly, every log and bush. She dodged
the brambles and jumped over a fallen branch,
sending puffs of snow flying.

[12] Foxes have excellent hearing and a very good sense of
smell. This helps them find prey, even under the snow.

Past the malthouse they ran, alongside the beehives covered in frost[13] and through the rose garden. In the courtyard, Tally stopped to catch her breath. 'I think we're safe now,' she said, gulping in frozen air until her chest hurt. 'Oh, that poor mouse!' Squill trembled and Tally stroked his fur.

The clock chimed from the house. It was quarter to midnight.

'Quick! To our hiding place! Madame Sage will be here any moment.'

[13] In the winter, the honey bees huddle around the queen to keep her warm. The bees shiver their wings to make heat.

CHAPTER EIGHT

Tally crept into the ballroom, her night goggles in her hand. Luckily Mrs Sneed had already told her to keep out of sight, so no one would notice Tally was gone.

She fiddled with the teeny dial on the wall, turning it:

left one click,

right three clicks,

left four clicks.

The door clicked open and Tally climbed inside the small cupboard, goggles in hand. Squill jumped up after her and settled in her lap. Tally pulled the door closed. It was dark in here. Pitch black. She couldn't see a thing!

She fitted the leather strap of the night goggles over her ears. She closed her eyes for a moment and, when she opened them, she could make out the stone walls of the cupboard, the bumps and lumps of the uneven surface.

She didn't have to wait very long. There was a noise from the ballroom door.

'Everyone wait here while I check the room,' said a soft floaty voice.

'It's Madame Sage,' Tally whispered.

There was a squeak of old wood – the sound of a window being opened. Then the *click click* of the curtains being pulled closed, and the *tappity-tap* of heels, as Madame Sage walked back to the centre of the room.

'Come in,' said Madame Sage in a singsong way.

Tally heard the scrape of chairs on the marble floor as everyone took their places. Squill's ears pricked up.

They were both ready – ready to see what Madame Sage would do.

'Ooooh,' Madame Sage sang, 'I can feel the spirits waiting nearby.'

From the hidey-hole, Tally heard the muffled sound of Lady Beatrice's gasp.

'They were not happy in the night,' said Madame Sage.

'Goodness!' cried Mrs Sneed, in her sharp, spiky voice. 'How did she know that?'

'She must be psychic,' came Mr Bood's rich deep tones.

'Spirits? Yes!' cried Lady Beatrice breathlessly. 'I heard them groaning in the night! Can you make them go away? Please? I've got this for you.' There was a clatter as coins spilled on to the wooden table.

'Well, that's a start,' said Madame Sage. 'Now, it's time to turn out the lamps. Then the spirits will come forth.'

Tally squeezed Squill's paw. She could hear Mr Bood as he clomped around the ballroom, extinguishing the lamps.

'It's gone dark!' cried Lady Beatrice, finally

realising what was going to happen when the lamps were out.

'I can't see a thing. It's total darkness,' said Mrs Sneed.

'Good, that's what I ne— I mean, that's what the spirits need,' said Madame Sage quickly. Then her voice became low and singsong again. 'Come, spirits!' she warbled. 'Make yourselves known!'

Tally pushed the door of the hidey-hole open as slowly as possible, hoping that the little click couldn't be heard. She stayed in the hole, peeping out through the crack. The room was

very dark – the curtains had been pulled over the open window to hide the moonlight. But her night goggles showed her a grey, grainy scene. Now she could see, as well as hear, what was going on.

Five people sat at the table in the ballroom: Lord Mollett and Lady Beatrice, Mr Bood, Mrs Sneed and Madame Sage.

Lady Beatrice was wearing a long black gown decorated with silver stars she'd stuck on all by herself. Every time she moved another one peeled off at the edges and dropped on the floor. Balanced on her hat was a huge butterfly net with which, she'd told Tally earlier, 'I'll be able to trap the ghosts!'

She also had some earrings she'd asked Tally to make her out of two cloves of garlic – just in case it was vampires, not ghosts. On the table was her beloved camera.

'Come forth!' wailed Madame Sage. 'I call you here!' She blew on a whistle and everyone jumped.

A grey shape slipped through the curtains into the room. *The opossum!* It ran straight to Madame Sage's open palm, held out low next to the table. The opossum took a treat from Madame Sage's hand. She waved him away and pointed at the other end of the ballroom.

The opossum ran all the way there. He lifted his head. **Gʀoooooooo**, he growled.

'OH!' cried Lady Beatrice. 'The groaning noise!'

Gʀooooooo

'What do you want, spirit?' asked Madame Sage.

'Yes, what do they want?' said Lady Beatrice.

'What's that, spirits? What do you say?' Madame Sage went on.

'What do they say, Madame Sage?' Lady Beatrice begged.

'Well, they say you should give me more money for all the hard work I'm doing,' said Madame Sage rather matter-of-factly. And continuing in her faraway voice, she said, 'Then they will be appeased.'

Without a second thought Lady Beatrice handed over another pile of coins: *clink, clink, clink.*

In the darkness, Madame Sage waved her hand again and the opossum ran back for another treat. **Gʀoooooooo** went the noise.

Clink clink clink went the sound of coins from Lady Beatrice's purse.

Tally grew more and more cross. That woman was tricking Lady Beatrice out of her money! She itched to jump out and stop it all. But she waited, waited for the right moment.

Groooooooo went the noise again.

'Goodness! My purse is empty,' said Lady Beatrice. She took off her necklace and put it in Madame Sage's waiting palm. 'That's it. I have nothing left. Please just tell the spirits to go,' she sobbed.

'There's always your camera, m'lady,' suggested Mr Bood, unhelpfully.

From the cubbyhole Tally could see Madame Sage tilt her head to the side, remembering Lady Beatrice's top-of-the-range camera, so smart and fancy, rich polished wood and shiny brass.

'Yeeees,' said Madame Sage slowly, 'that might do for me— I mean, for the spirits.'

'Oh but ...' In the dark Lady Beatrice felt for the camera and held it to her chest. 'I couldn't possibly ... this camera ... it's my future, my craft ...'

'Yes, Beatrice – please don't give her your camera,' Lord Mollett said firmly.

'It's up to you, of course.' Madame Sage waved her hand airily. 'It depends whether you want to get rid of the spirits or not.'

'I do! But my camera …'

'What's that?' Madame Sage said in a sharp voice. Everyone jumped. 'A spirit wants to make itself known!' She waved the opossum over and, quick as she could, threw a little sheet over him. 'Oh yes, I can sense it arriving …'

Madame Sage swiftly rose from the table and walked to the window. She yanked back the curtain. The moon bathed the floor in soft grey light. 'Open your eyes!' cried Madame Sage. There on the ballroom floor was a small figure all in white.

Lady Beatrice's resolve crumbled as she screamed 'Take my camera!', pushing it across the table towards Madame Sage.

Tally seized her moment. She pulled off her night goggles and burst out of the hidey-hole.

'Hold it right there!' she cried loudly. Quick as

133

she could, she lit the lamp.

The ballroom was flooded in light. Everyone blinked.

'Tally?' said Lord Mollett in confusion. 'What are you doing here?'

'This woman is a trickster and a thief!' cried Tally, running towards the window. 'There are no ghosts. Meet Madame Sage's accomplice!'

She pulled the sheet off the figure. On the floor stood a small grey creature, balancing on its hind legs.

Lady Beatrice gasped.

Tally scooped up the opossum. He wriggled in her hand, big eyes blinking in the light.

'It was this opossum who made the groaning noise. He's the one who scared you in the night. They've tricked you!'

'I think I'll be going now,' said Madame Sage primly and stepped towards the door. 'I know when I'm not wanted.'

'Sit back down, Madame Sage,' Tally said with authority. 'I've only just begun.' She paced across the floor with the opossum in her arms. Five faces watched her from the table.

'My suspicions were first aroused when I found

footprints on Lady Beatrice's window sills,' said Tally. 'I knew there was no ghost. It was clear that something real was scaring her.'

'Humph,' said Madame Sage, folding her arms. 'I didn't promise there were ghosts.'

Tally ignored her. 'I noticed the footprints were of small hand-like paws. Paws like this!' Tally turned one of the opossum's feet so everyone could see the base.

'Then I found fur in two locations, first in straw in the stables, and second on the drainpipe going up to Lady Beatrice's room. Grey fur. Just like this.' She pointed at the opossum's coat.

'That proves nothing,' said Madame Sage, taking her pet from Tally. 'Lots of creatures have grey fur.'

'So I knew I was looking for a creature that has hand-like paws and grey fur. And then, when Madame Sage arrived, I noticed two things. Firstly: Madame Sage had straw caught on her shoe – straw from the stable, the place where the creature had made a temporary nest. Secondly: she brought a basket with her, a basket William liked to sniff. A basket large enough to carry a small animal. A basket that was full when she first arrived – and empty when she left!'

Everyone gasped.

'And last night I saw the very creature I was

looking for – this opossum.'

Tally turned to Madame Sage. 'You let him loose in the manor house, didn't you?'

Madame Sage bristled. 'It's not my fault he got out of the basket.'

'You chose a nocturnal creature on purpose,' Tally continued.

'Knock knock'll?' said Mr Bood, puzzled. 'What does that mean?'

'I think she said "not normal",' Mrs Sneed explained.

'Yes!' said Lady Beatrice firmly, getting into the spirit of Tally's big reveal. 'Madame Sage, you chose a not normal creature on purpose!'

'Nocturnal,' said Tally gently. 'It means a creature that is active at night-time. My guess is that Madame Sage made a plan. A plan to target someone emotionally vulnerable. Someone with a past they were ashamed of. Someone she'd read about in the newspaper.'

She turned to Madame Sage. 'You knew of Lady Beatrice's history. You knew she was fragile and lonely. So you sent your pet to scare her at night. You trained him to tap on her windows. Then you sent her your calling card. You knew she'd invite you inside the house, and, the moment she did you let your pet loose to cause even more upset – groaning and growling through the night.' Tally shook her head. 'All this to trick her out of her coins and nearly out of her valuable camera.'

Madame Sage huffed. 'I would have got away with it if it hadn't been for this pesky child.'

Lady Beatrice looked shocked. 'I want my money back,' she said firmly, retrieving her camera from the table and holding out her palm.

The medium was furious. She glowered at Tally, her eyes narrowed as she handed back every coin she'd stolen, and the necklace.

'Mr Bood – telephone the police,' said Lord Mollett. 'This is the last time Madame Sage will trick anyone.'

Madame Sage scowled. The opossum climbed back into the empty basket, where it was nice and dark.

'Well done, Tally,' said Lord Mollett, turning

to her. 'You saved us again.'

Mrs Sneed sniffed.

'I always thought there was something fishy …
er, I mean, opossum-y about that woman,' said
Mr Bood.

Tally hid her smile.

'We're all going to sleep a lot better tonight,'
Lord Mollett declared.

And they did.

CHAPTER 9

The next morning the manor house was back to normal.

Mrs Sneed was snoozing by the fire.

Mr Bood was making a list of chores.

1. Chores for Twooly to do
Stop snow falling on roses
Warm up lawn
Make sun shine

2. Chores for me to do
Brush hair in case of photos

Meanwhile, having solved one mystery, Tally still had another one to investigate.

She was pretending to sweep Lord Mollett's

room, but really she was looking for Ma's letter. She searched the floorboards by his window, in case it had fallen down a crack in the wood. She searched under his bed, in case it had been blown there. She ran her fingers over every bump in the stone wall, in case it had got caught in a hidden opening. Nothing.

She heard a sniffing from the room opposite. It was Lady Beatrice. She was very upset.

'Are you OK?' Tally asked, moving to the doorway of her room.

'Oh, Tally. I'm just so silly. I can't believe that woman tricked me!'

Tally crossed the room and touched her arm. 'She was very devious,' she said. 'She tricked everyone.'

'Not you,' said Lady Beatrice. She stood up and walked to the window. 'I wasn't always like this, Tally. I used to be a happy thing. When the duke proposed to me, I was so excited. I couldn't believe he had noticed me. Even if he was a bit bossy and annoying, I didn't mind. I was going to be a duchess! Everyone was so impressed. But then, then when he broke off the engagement, they all stopped talking to me. And I began to wonder if it really was all my fault.' She sniffed. 'Since then I've felt like I couldn't do anything. Couldn't become anything.'

Tally wasn't sure what to say. Mrs Sneed's words came back to her: *We were none of us quite ourselves after that.*

'In the summer I thought I was getting better.' Lady Beatrice drew two little eyes in the condensation on the window. 'With William, and my camera, I felt like I was slowly waking up again, returning to my normal self. But now, all those sleepless nights have ruined my work, and made me mess up the only paid job I've had.' She added a sad mouth to her picture. 'Now I fear I'll never be a proper photographer.'

The gate bell rang. Tally ran to the window and saw the postman standing at the gate with a large parcel.

'It's your photographs, Lady Beatrice,' said

Tally. 'They're back from the factory.'

'That's what I was afraid of. There's not much point in opening them.' Lady Beatrice sighed. 'They're bound to be all wrong. I was so tired when I took them. Please get me some tea, will you, dear?'

'Hold on. I'll be right back,' Tally said. She ran downstairs and across the courtyard. Widdles was already at the gate.

'Wuff!' He loved the postman. The postman had very tasty trousers.

'Off him, Widdles!' said Tally, pulling the puppy away.

She took the parcel into the kitchen. Widdles jumped up to sniff it. 'No. Photos are not edible, Widdles,' said Tally. He looked so disappointed that

Tally gave him one of her biscuits.

'Ruff!' he said, gobbling it down happily.

'Let's take some biscuits up for Lady Beatrice with her tea. That might cheer her up.' Squill counted out some cherry biscuits on to a plate while Tally got a tray.

She carried the parcel and biscuits carefully up the stairs, Widdles running in circles around her.

Tally sat down next to Lady Beatrice on the chaise longue.

'Let's see,' Tally said gently. She opened the envelope, slipping the photographs out. She held her breath – hopefully one or two would have come out. She looked down and gasped. 'These are good!' she cried.

Lady Beatrice sat up. 'Really?'

'Yes!' Tally spread them out on the low table. They were black and white photographs of the courtyard – clear and neat and not blurry at all. But Lady Beatrice hadn't just taken well-focused images of Widdles. She'd cleverly caught the sparkle of the water in the fountain, the shape of a leaf on the white snow, the contrast of light and shade on the cobblestones. She seemed to have captured the atmosphere of the manor perfectly. They were indeed wonderful pictures – even if Mr Bood's gurning face appeared in a few too many of them.

'Oh … oh …' Lady Beatrice turned pink with happiness. 'These have come out well, haven't they?'

'They really have,' said Tally warmly, and Lady Beatrice smiled.

'Let's see the one of Lord William looking elegant.' Lady Beatrice shuffled through the pictures till she came to the puppy shots.

Um. There was Widdles, clumps of mud in his fur, a dribble of sticks in his mouth and a mad look of glee on his face. Tally froze. Was Lady Beatrice going to burst into tears again?

'He looks wonderful!' she cried. 'What a handsome puppy!'

'Wuff!' agreed Widdles from the bed, where he'd trodden melted snow across the sheets, and was chewing the pillow. 'Ruff!' A flurry of feathers puffed out of his mouth.

'The publisher is going to love these,' said Lady Beatrice. 'You know, Tally, I've had enough of feeling sorry for myself. I'm not a silly thing. I'm a photographer. A talented photographer. A proper photographer. And that's what I'm going to be from now on.'

She took a bite of biscuit. 'I am not a silly thing,' she repeated. 'Mmm. How did you make these, Tally?'

'Well,' said Tally, 'you take some flour and butter and – do stop me if this gets complicated – you mix them together in a bowl—'

'Stop!' cried Lady Beatrice.

The letter wasn't in Lord Mollett's room – not in the floorboards, not in the cracks, not in the fireplace, nor attached to the back of his

collection of paintings of native British birds wearing pyjamas (which had been rejected by the Royal Academy Summer Exhibition for being 'not sufficiently sensible').

Where was Ma's letter?

Tally slumped down on to the hallway floor.

She only had Ma's diary, and that wouldn't prove anything. Outside of the Secret Library the magic wouldn't work – Ma's hologram wouldn't appear and there would only be her written words.

Tally frowned, picturing what Ma had written:

'The Mollett family! They'll never accept it – not from a village girl.

I won't tell anyone. It will be my secret.'

She could have screamed in frustration. Without seeing Ma's hand stroking the baby in her belly, the words were meaningless. And Tally couldn't take Lord Mollett to the library, even if she wanted to break her vow of secrecy. He was definitely older than thirteen! The trapdoor wouldn't open for him.

'I'll never find the letter,' Tally whispered. 'I'll never be able to prove any of it.'

It's for the best.

A tear slid down her cheek. Squill gave a soft sigh. He curled his little paws around her wrist and laid his head on her hand. Tally sniffed.

'Let's go to the Secret Library, Squill. It's the only place that can make me feel better.'

In the library, Tally couldn't resist opening the diary again for one more look at Ma. She turned the page to the last entry and read it out loud again.

'I left Bear the letter.'

Ma appeared, standing on the cliffs.

'But, just as I dropped it into his window, someone appeared and I had to rush away or risk being caught!'

The scene switched again to show the dark room.

'Oh, I wish I could see!' cried Tally. 'But it's too dark.'

She slumped her chin on to her upturned palms and sighed. Squill cuddled up next to her, and they sat there in silence for a moment.

'Wait, wait – too dark?'
She gave a sharp laugh.
'Oh, Squill, I'm so silly!
Of course I can see it – I
have these!' She held up
her night vision goggles.
Fingers trembling, she
pulled them over her head.
Then she read Ma's words
again.

The hologram shimmered,
and an image came to life.

With the goggles Tally could see the room
clearly!

It *was* Lord Mollett's bedroom, with his red
velvet curtains. The room was empty, but just
outside the window was Ma, balancing on a
branch. A handwritten letter lay on the wooden
floor, resting on one of the floorboards. Tally
squinted to try to see it better, but it was too
small. There was a tap of shoes. Ma shrank
back into the branches just as someone entered
the room.

It was a woman, a young woman. There was something familiar about her …

'It's Mrs Sneed!' cried Tally. 'Mrs Sneed when she was younger.'

In the hologram, Mrs Sneed cracked her neck to the side and reached down to pick up the letter. She held her back as she did so, wincing as if in pain. Tally blinked. She'd never known that Mrs Sneed's back hurt her. Tally had always thought the housekeeper was simply lazy.

Tally could just about make out Ma's writing on the letter, but not what it said. Mrs Sneed looked at the letter and shrugged, shoving it carelessly into her pocket. She couldn't read it.

'That can't be it!' Tally cried. The library was suddenly cold. 'This can't be the end, Ma's letter just a piece of paper to be thrown away!'

She read Ma's diary again, slowly this time, looking for clues. The hologram responded, moving the scene as if playing it in slow motion. There! There was the moment Mrs Sneed turned the paper over. Tally peered closer. There was a drawing on the back of the paper. Tally paused in her reading. Something about it looked familiar but it was so small in the hologram, Tally couldn't make it out.

With a cry Tally reached for the glass bottle of water she kept by the blanket. Tally held it up to her goggles and looked through the water. From behind the glass the library shelves were distorted. They curved around in strange ways, in and out of focus, some huge and some small.[14] She angled the glass till it was right where the hologram appeared and, with a quick glance down, read Ma's sentence again. The moment Mrs Sneed turned the paper, Tally adjusted the bottle. The image grew larger, fuzzy and distorted, but bigger.

'Oh!' Tally cried. She knew! She knew where she'd seen that drawing before! It was an illustration of a little biscuit.

[14] As light travels through the glass bottle of water, it bends from its usual path. So when Tally looks at the letter through her glass bottle, the bending light makes the letter look bigger. You can try this yourself with a jar of water.

Tally and Squill raced across the snowy garden, past the apple orchard, through the frosty roses and over the cloister to the back door of Mollett Manor. Her heart was beating so fast it was nearly bursting out of her chest, and her throat felt tight.

Ma's letter had been here all along!

She flung open the back door and skidded on the stone floor as she ran to the kitchen.

There on the wall was the recipe for Lord Mollett's favourite biscuits, the ingredients written by hand. On the top of the paper was a little illustration for the cook, a drawing of what the biscuits would look like. Mrs Sneed might not have been able to read, but she knew what biscuits looked like. She'd stuck the recipe up here on the wall all those years ago.

Gently, Tally pulled the recipe from where it had lived these past twelve years. She turned over the paper and, on the back, was the letter:

Darling Bear,
I have to go. They are taking me away.
I have so much to tell you and so little time.

We are going to have a baby! They want me to give it up, but I won't. I'm going to keep it and one day, when I'm older, when they can't stop me, I am going to come back and find you.

Wait for me! Wait for our baby.

In the meantime — here is the recipe for your favourite biscuits. Eat them and think of me.

I love you,

Your Martha

This was it: proof Ma and Edward had had a baby! Now all she had to do was show Lord Mollett the letter and …

… *wait.*

A chill ran through Tally.

She could prove Lord Mollett and Ma had a baby but not that she was the baby. Not that she was his daughter. All she had was a scrap of lace hidden in her sleeve – but that could

have come from anyone's skirt. Why should he believe her?

'Tally?' Lord Mollett's voice rang through the manor. 'I need your help with this last chapter!'

Tally froze. The letter felt heavy in her hand.

'Should I tell him?' she whispered.

Squill jumped from the kitchen counter to land on her shoulder. He rested his little head against her cheek. He felt so soft and warm. Tally pressed her cheek back against him.

She had no idea what to do.

CHAPTER TEN

What should I do what should I do what should I do what should I do what should I do what should I do?

The question repeated over and over in Tally's head. Every step she took, every step across the stone hallway and up the stairs to the study, seemed to echo with the phrase.

Tally touched the letter in her pinafore pocket. *It's for the best.*

Would he want a daughter? Would he want Tally?

Her hand lifted, curled in a fist to knock at the

study door. She glanced at Squill, perched on her shoulder. He nibbled one of her curls in support. Tally nodded. Lord Mollett deserved to know that Ma had written to him and that there was a child, even if Tally couldn't prove she was that child. And even if he didn't want one.

She tapped at the door and pushed it open.

'Ah, there you are,' said Lord Mollett warmly. 'I've been waiting for you.' He smiled at her. 'Tally? Are you OK? You're very pale. Here. Sit down.' Lord Mollett led her to a chair by the fire and sat down opposite her.

Tally pulled the letter from her pocket. 'I … I found something,' she said. 'It was on the back of that biscuit recipe.'

'I love those cherry biscuits!' said Lord Mollett cheerfully. 'Someone used to make them for me long ago.' He took his glasses out of his waistcoat pocket and put them on.

His head was bowed, reading the letter for a long time. When he finished, Tally could see his eyes moving back to the top so he could read it all over again. Finally, he lifted his head, tears rolling down his cheeks.

'Martha!' His eyes shone through the tears. 'She *did* love me! She didn't leave me. Oh, poor Martha.' He stood up. 'I must find her, Tally. I'll tell you all about her, then you can help me.

There are bound to be records! We can get her address.' He stopped and stared at Tally in excitement. 'A child! I have a child!'

Her stomach clenched tight. *What should I do what should I do?*

Lord Mollett frowned. 'I wonder why Martha didn't come back?' He stared out of the window. 'Maybe she forgot.' His voice became lighter, more shaky. 'Maybe she found someone else.'

Tally stood sharply. She couldn't let him think that. 'She *did* come back,' she said clearly. Lord Mollett turned to look at her, confusion on his face.

'Nine years ago she came here to Mollett Manor. She came to find you.'

'I don't understand …'

Tears prickled at the back of Tally's eyes. 'She came with her daughter. She meant to see you but first … first she wanted to fetch something. Her old diary.'

'She always wrote in a diary,' said Lord Mollett. 'How do you …'

Tally could just remember it – flashes of images, like photographs, came back to her.

'This way, darling,' Ma had whispered. 'Nice and quiet now. We're not really supposed to be here.'

She was so close to crying. But she had to get the story out. Lord Mollett deserved to know. She swallowed hard and continued to talk, her voice almost mechanical. 'She went to the cliff edge, to the hole where it was hidden.'

It had been windy that day – Ma had laughed as it nearly blew her hat away. Tally could see her, grinning into the wind. Ma had reached down, leaning over the edge of the cliff. The wind blew and Ma stumbled. Tally grabbed for her, her little fingers grasping the hem of Ma's skirt.

'… and she was gone.' It nearly broke Tally to say it. 'Gone over the cliff.'

Lord Mollett took a step closer. 'How do you know all that, Tally?'

'Because … Because …' Her voice was hoarse. 'Martha – she was my mother.' Tally burst into tears. Her words came out through sobs, hiccupping. 'I know I can't prove it. I know you have no reason to believe me. But she really was my mother.' Tally pulled out the tiny bit of lace from Ma's skirt. 'And this is almost all I have left of her.' She handed Lord Mollett the precious scrap and buried her head in her arms, crying and crying.

Lord Mollett could have asked for more details.

He could have interrogated Tally further.

He could have taken a while to think about this news.

But he didn't hesitate for a moment.

Warm arms surrounded Tally, as he scooped her up.

'You don't need to prove it,' he said.

Tally froze, waiting to hear his next words.

'I believe you.'

Tally's heart felt like it might lift her into the air and up out of the window. She put her arms round her father and held on so tight. Squill jumped up, eager not to be left out. He landed on

Tally's head and put his paw on Lord Mollett's forearm.

Lord Mollett set her down and looked at her closely. 'I should have realised.' He shook his head at his own foolishness. 'You have her eyes. And, more than that, you have her clever brain. Martha was just like you, Tally. She was always the first with an idea, the first to fix a problem, to solve a mystery. That's why I loved her. Oh, Tally – I'm so happy you are here!'

'But you said … you said it was good that you hadn't had children, that it was for the best.'

'I didn't mean it like that,' said Lord Mollett. 'I only meant that I had to make the best of the life that I was living. A life with no wife. And no child. I suppose I was just trying to cheer myself up. But now – now you're here. And it's so, so wonderful!' He ran a hand through his hair, suddenly shy.

Tally grinned at him.

'We've got a lot to do,' said Lord Mollett all in a rush. 'Together, you and I, we're going to find out what happened to Martha.'

Tally breathed in. It was her turn to believe.

'But first,' he said, 'first we're going to tell everyone about the new lady of the manor!'

'Lady?' said Tally, puzzled.

'Oh yes. You're Lady Tallulah Mollett now,' said her father. 'I have a daughter, and I want the whole world to know.'

Acknowledgements

My thanks go: to Lena McCauley and the
team; to James Brown for his fantastic
illustrations; and, as always, to my wonderful
agent Eve White.

I also want to mention the Hawk and Owl Trust,
who (very patiently) explained precisely how an
owl can sleep standing up.
— Abie Longstaff

ABOUT THE AUTHOR

ABIE LONGSTAFF is the eldest of six children
and grew up in Australia, Hong Kong and
France. She knows all about squabbling and
bossing younger sisters around so she began her
career as a barrister. She started writing when
her children were born. Her books include
The Fairytale Hairdresser series and *The Magic
Potions Shop* books. She has a life-long love of
fairy tales and mythology and her work is greatly
influenced by these themes.

Abie got the idea for *The Trapdoor Mysteries*
from her parents' house in France. The house is
big and old, with lots of rooms and outbuildings.
In one of the bedrooms, there is a secret entrance
hidden in a fireplace. It leads to a room that was
used by the French Resistance during the war. It
was the perfect idea for a book!

Abie lives with her family by the seaside in Hove.

ABOUT THE ILLUSTRATOR

Inspired by a school visit from Anthony Browne at the age of eight, JAMES BROWN has wanted to illustrate ever since. Having won the SCBWI's Undiscovered Voices 2014 competition, he had illustrated the *Elspeth Hart* series and two of his own *Archie and George* books. Two picture books he has written, *With My Mummy* and *With My Daddy*, are recently published and his first author-illustrator picture book, *Jingle Spells*, is out as well. He is the illustrator for the new *Al's Awesome Science* series. James comes from Nottingham and has two cheeky daughters who usually take off with his favourite crayons.

FIND OUT WHAT HAPPENS IN
TALLY AND SQUILL'S FINAL ADVENTURE . . .

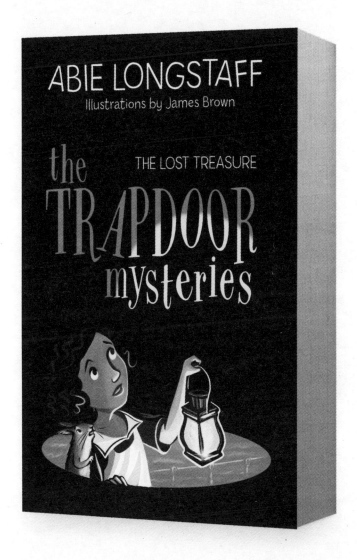

ABIE LONGSTAFF
Illustrations by James Brown

THE LOST TREASURE

the
TRAPDOOR
mysteries